Blanket Of Deception

BLANKET OF DECEPTION

Blanket of Deception

A Novel

Joe C. DeAguero

BLANKET OF DECEPTION

Copyright © 2012 by
Joe C. DeAguero
All rights reserved

This is wholly a work of fiction. Any resemblance of characters to actual persons, living, dead or undead or almost dead is purely coincidental. Cultural, spiritual and religious references were created as a work of fiction and no disrespect is intended. If you are offended, please consult your physician or mental health provider, as the reader assumes full responsibility when reading works of fiction. Unauthorized duplication is strictly prohibited. If rash, irritation, or swelling develops, discontinue reading. Not intended as a flotation device or a napalm igniter, unless absolutely necessary.

ISBN – 13: 978-0615645728
ISBN – 10: 0615645728

Author Photo by Karen DeAguero
Cover Design by Joe C. DeAguero and
Joan Madsen of jcreative
Background Photograph by
Joe C. DeAguero

Image of Native American by:
Edward S. Curtis (1868-1952)
Crying To The Spirits, 1908
Northwestern University Library, *Edward S. Curtis's 'The North American Indian" the Photographic Images, 2001.*
http://memory.loc.gov/ammem/award98/ienhtml/curthome.html

Special thanks to

Dean Metcalf
Author of Rattlesnake Dreams:
An American Warrior's Story
for his wisdom, encouragement, and friendship.

and

Jon Rombach
Writer, journalist and good friend for his
exceptional insight and keen perspective.
Jonrombach.com

*To my love Mary Catherine
and our warm-hearted daughter
Karen Rebecca*

i	Words Of Heinmot Tooyalaket	8
ii	Native American Prayer	9
iii	My Belief	10
1	You Will Endure	11
2	Closed Eyes	16
3	A Clear Understanding	24
4	Two Spirit Worlds	40
5	The Cross	45
6	Old Bones	53
7	Cowboys and Peaceful Nights	63
8	Yellow Eyed Dog	71
9	Load Up	78
10	Ten Rules	85
11	Uncommon Good Will	96
12	Nal-Geen Bottle	100
13	Precious Blue Stone	105
14	The Offer	116
15	Yellow Canines	121
16	Melancholy Rain	125
17	Moonlight Bounce	129
18	Dream Of A White Spider	136
19	Shadow People	143
20	Sacred Thunderbird	150
21	The Sins Of Others	162
22	Crimson	169
23	Bitter As Blood	174
24	The People's Congress	182
25	One Spirit	188
26	Gray Shadowed Thunderbird	195
27	Amelia's Chess Game	202
28	Deep Investigations	215
29	Spiritual Premonition	226
30	Silky Gray Mist	235
31	Religion	242
32	Burning Salt Bed	248
33	Still Waters	274

i   Words Of Heinmot Tooyalaket

The earth was created by the assistance of the sun, and it should be left as it was.... The Country was made without lines of demarcation and it is no mans business to divide it.... I see the whites all over the country gaining wealth and see their desire to give us lands, which are worthless.

The earth and myself are of one mind. The measure of land and the measure of our bodies are the same. Say it to us if you can say it, that you were sent by Creative Power to talk to us. Perhaps you think the creator sent you here to destroy us as you see fit. If I thought you were sent by the creator I might be induced to think you had a right to dispose of me.

Do not misunderstand me, but understand me fully with reference to my affection to the land. I never said the land was mine to do with as I chose. The one who has a right to dispose of it is the one who has created it. I claim a right to live on my land, and accord you the privilege to live on yours.
Heinmot Tooyalaket,
Chief Joseph - Nez Perce

ii Native American Prayer

Oh our Mother the Earth, Oh our Father the Sky, your children are we, and with tired backs we bring you the gifts you love.
Then weave for us a garment of brightness;
May the warp be the white light of the morning,
May the weft be the red light of the evening,
May the fringes be the falling rain,
May the border be the standing rainbow.
Thus weave for us a garment of brightness, that we may walk fittingly where birds sing,
That we may walk fitting where grass is green,
Oh our Mother Earth, Oh our Father Sky.

iii   My belief

I trust,
but not everyone
I believe,
but not everyone
I love,
but not everyone
I tolerate,
but not everything
I smile,
from the depth of the soul
I play,
with childlike exuberance
I work,
with true purpose
I give,
when it is right
I question Everything,
because I Must

1   You Will Endure

Above all, don't lie to yourself. The man who lies to himself and listens to his own lie comes to a point that he cannot distinguish the truth within him, or around him, and so loses all respect for himself and for others. And having no respect he ceases to love.
Fyodor Dostoyevsky - The Brothers Karamazov

A vivid crimson and coral sunset filtered through the dense canopy of trees near Kawana Bay on the south shore of Oneida Lake, New York. The sinew was drawn taught around the wrists and ankles of Jack Burton. Jack had just been named the U.S. Secretary of State's Energy Director and was being shackled by five men dressed in animal hides. Painted faces hid their eyes, and they wore dark brown capes that draped down past their knees. The cloaked men moved about in quick, awkward gaits. The manner in which they tied Jack's wrists, then ankles, was methodical and unyielding, cutting the circulation to his hands and feet. Jack didn't know how he had ended up in this wooded area. His last recollection was that he was at his new office waiting on the computer tech to finish his network protocols and assist him with the initial set up. He had a migraine from the gin martini he had over lunch with his new boss, U.S. Secretary Vance. Gin had never agreed with him, but she had insisted on a drink after lunch and he obliged her request. Jack had taken three aspirin from the pill bottle in his leather brief case and swallowed them dry. He recalled he was sweating profusely for reasons he could not clearly understand. His hands were sticky, his skin clammy and his right eye twitched, as it often did when he was under stress. Jack had walked out to the granite balcony of his office as the computer tech worked. Jack remembered that he didn't feel much better outside in the sweltering afternoon heat. At 5:03 the tech finished his work with a rapid fire of staccato key strokes.

"Mr. Burton, I'm done. You're all set up and connected to the network as you requested." There was no reply from Jack. Again the tech called out.

"Mr. Burton?" Again, no reply. The tech dismissed the fact that Jack was gone. He put his laptop in its black padded case and locked the office door as he exited.

Jack felt the strong lashing of sinew strapped around his chest as he was fastened onto a bark-covered post. The small sharp knots of broken-off branches pierced his head, back, and calve. He struggled to get loose, but his efforts just seemed to tighten the sinew further. He heard the men speak in a native tongue he recognized but it was somehow different, more primitive than the Oneida language he was accustom to. The men stood the post upright in a waiting hole which left his feet hanging two feet above the ground. He could make out the scarlet clouds of the setting sun through the limbs of the tall trees. The weight of his body rested on a broken branch that dug roughly into his groin. The caped men put stones in the hole to secure the post. They amassed dried leaves, twigs and then larger branches beneath him. Jack began to scream. The oldest man with deep wrinkles, dark eyes, and long stringy hair, had a look of profound disdain as he pointed with two fingers in a downward hooked motion. The leanest and strongest of the five men took Jack by the jaw causing his mouth to open wide. The muscular man grabbed a handful of owl feathers from a leather pouch tied at his waist and stuffed them in Jack's mouth to silence his screams. He tried to spit them out, but could not. Jack took harsh breaths through his nose like a hard-ridden horse. His eyes were wide with the horror knowing what was coming.

Once they had prepared Jack for his death, the old man with dark eyes approached and glared at him. The other four powerfully built men stood as if sculpted in bronze.

BLANKET OF DECEPTION

"You lie. You will endure as we have endured." The old man spoke to Jack in broken English. As he spoke, the old, man rapidly pointed to each the four men standing. He then stepped back and gestured to the men to start the fire. Two men knelt and with a rotating rod, started a slow smoldering fire. Again, Jack tried to yell out only to find his screams of fear were futile and eerily quiet. The fire smoldered slowly. It was a small, hot and vile. The smoke first burnt Jacks eyes and nose as he struggled to avoid the sting. Jack felt the searing heat of cinders below his feet. He could smell the stench of burning hair from his legs and eventually felt the immense pain that became unending. Jack would pass in and out of consciousness as his feet slowly blistered, then cooked the skin, flesh and bone until the marrow boiled, spewing downward from his charred legs. The old man with the dark eyes let Jack Burton burn slow. They watched in silence. The smell of cooking flesh and boiled blood filled the air that emanated from the embers below Jack. More than two hours elapsed then with a single rasping last gasp of air his bloodshot eyes opened wide and his entire body fell limp. The five men remained unmoved as they watched the last few drops of blood fall.

Green leaves were amassed on the remaining embers so Jack could be easily found. The five caped men then disappeared through the forest in a ghostlike rush of wind that shattered the silence of dusk.

2   Closed Eyes

The ground on which we stand is sacred ground. It is the blood of our ancestors.
Chief Plenty Coups - Crow

Saturday morning Father Ricardo Fernando de Herrera awoke. His sleeping room was dark with slivers of early light coming through the shuttered window. The room felt of winter. He rubbed his eyes, lifted off the heavy woolen blanket and started his day. He shuffled to his poorly lit kitchen to make his customary four cups of black Colombian coffee. He poured the water into the waiting pot, scooped in two tablespoons of ground coffee, and put the pot to heat on the old two-burner gas stove. Seated on the worn pine bench near the south-facing window, he silently watched as the haughty blue jays and chubby pumpkin colored robins pecked at specks of grain too minute to be seen. He suspected they were eating the leftover seed he had thrown the evening prior. The birds pecked, posed, and fluttered in their morning dance. When the coffee was brewed, he poured a black cupful. The thick, white ceramic cup was a favorite of his, as it was a gift ten years before from his friend Jackson Red Heart. Jackson was the great, great grandson of

Nez Perce Chief Ollokut, brother of Chief Joseph. Holding the cup firmly in both hands, he stood and watched out the window. He took a sip of the steaming, dark brew then left the birds to their revelry. Father Herrera went down the steps of the unlit narrow hallway towards his dim study to prepare for the day's prayers.

After his morning coffee and bird watching ritual, he worked in his stark study of the church. The room had the odor of time and dusty book stacks. Father Herrera knelt on the timeworn wood altar at the base of a shrine. It creaked with age as he knelt. Above him was a large saintly gesso statue of her holiness, Santa Maria, Madre de Dios, commonly known as Saint Mary. The saint was adorned in an ornate blue shawl with a shimmering gold hem. At her feet were several rows of small white and red candles at various stages of consumption. This minimal light made it possible to read from his Holy Book. As he knelt, he read his traditional morning prayers making a slow sign of the cross at the end of each prayer with his right hand before turning to the next. When the morning sacrament was complete, he stood, blew out the candles and retreated to his study to prepare the sermon for the Sunday's mass. Father Herrera had been working on a sermon to share with his congregation on the importance of spiritual clarity and discovering your true self. The words for his sermon did not come easy. He struggled to impart the important message of spiritual certainty to the worshippers. Despite his trouble on this reflective topic, he valued the challenges in reaching this higher state of contemplation. He would share his insight with his congregation while honestly explaining his own shortcomings and divulging his own humility. He sincerely believed in the importance of a spiritually clear heart and mind. He took the last sip of coffee that long ago had become cold. The father mulled over his words and re-read them aloud as he shuffled down the bare hall to the now sunlit kitchen.

    Father Herrera felt the morning hours were always a good time to write and think though the issues that needed deep introspection. He again sat at the kitchen window. Watched the birds as they danced, turning their heads to listen to an insect, worm or what they found to be edible moving in the silvery dew on the morning grass. Ready to strike, they would listen, focus, and swiftly peck down on their morning meal. The birds would quickly gulp, shake off the dew, and again assume the position to listen, head cocked like a curious dog.

    Father Herrera struggled through his sermon. He spoke of a man who has the presence of mind to share insights and bring spiritual enlightenment to the soul. Not through the use of indoctrinations, but through the power of observation, reflection and a connection with a spiritual power. Some call it focus, to others it is meditation, mindfulness, or it may be called simple peacefulness. It was not the power of prayer nor the connection with the heavenly Father. Rather, it was the natural connection to the spirits that inhabit the earth. This greater power was purposeful and was a conscious relationship with Mother Earth. The man he spoke of was his friend Jackson Red Heart. Jackson was a deeply spiritual man who shared the ways of the earth with people who desired to find a clarity and calmness within themselves. This higher state of being could be found in nature and the natural spirits he believed exist in and of this earth. His insight into the natural world illustrated a way people could free themselves from their own perception of their jaded life. Commonly this would include people that lead their existence surrounded by concrete walls and roads and a prejudice mind. In his sermon he also spoke of being aware of the implication of choices. Daily decisions people make lead them down distinct roads, each with their own remarkable advantage and equally difficult consequences. Not all bad, not all good, just different roads and diverse experiences that make people whole. It was these journeys, experiences, and give souls their depth, character, spirit to remain hopeful. Father Herrera ended his sermon, and added that there would be a gathering for those interested in finding their inner spirit and truth that was within them. The presentation would be Tuesday at 7:00 p.m.

Tuesday evening, Father Herrera stood at the podium. Several of his parishioners listened with sincere interest as he introduced his long time friend, Jackson Red Heart. Jackson started with a short introduction telling of his boyhood. He spoke about living within the spiritual world that surrounded him, his village, and his native people. He then showed pictures of his living journeys, as he liked to describe them. The first photo was of a group of men and women standing atop a rocky mountain he called Eagle Cap Peak. The terrain shown was steep. Needle shaped crags were separated by broad green meadows and clusters of evergreen trees amongst the clear lakes. Each photo he showed was exceptionally scenic and filled with an aura of freedom only a wild place could bring. The onlookers could feel the clean, burning crispness of the air. After his introduction, Jackson showed a series of stunning wildlife photos. He spoke of the wildlife, their roles in nature including the spiritual meanings of the eagles, mule deer, elk, bear, and wolves. One of the photos showed a coyote concealed in the dense underbrush, peering out with his jovial yellow eyes. He spoke of the experiences other people had on previous trips. This included a young man whom he called Patrick. At the time he was twenty three and had been in and out of trouble since turning fifteen. Patrick was smart but had trouble seeing beyond today and lived for only the moment. After his trip to the wilderness, Patrick returned to his hometown of Hot Springs, South Dakota, which was near the Nebraska and Wyoming borders. There in the stillness of his small hometown, he reflected on his wilderness experience and found a clear path to follow. He joined the Peace Corps and traveled the world, helping people in need. Father Herrera said Patrick had visited with him about five months ago when he returned to the States. Patrick imparted that his life journey to the Eagle Cap Wilderness some nine years ago had given him the foundation for his life. He was endlessly grateful for his journey helped him connect to his soul and eternal life purpose.

Everyone there listened with great interest in finding a spiritual approach to a purposeful life. All except for the young lady in the back row of neatly aligned chairs. Dressed in skin tight blue denim jeans, an oversized navy colored hooded sweater and large white rimmed sunglasses, was Shelby Garrett. But she was not alone. Her sternly religious and often overbearing Mom, Joanne, was with her. Joanne was the reason Shelby attended Jackson's presentation. Joanne was intent on getting her only daughter to enlighten herself and to see that there was more to life. There was more to living than the drama of soap operas, loser boyfriends, and sleeping past noon. Shelby, however, had no intention of ever going on this so called wilderness life journey with Old Jackson, Jackie-Boy or whatever in hell his name was. No matter how heavenly and spiritual this journey was portrayed. Regardless of why her Mom would say she needed this experience, Shelby gave thought to the notion of no TV, no restaurants, no bed, no bars and no shower. No way!

Thirty minutes later, to Shelby's downright disbelief, her *beloved* Mother had her signed up for her very own wilderness experience. Joanne handed Jackson Shelby's $1,000 trip deposit. In return, Jackson gave Shelby a large colored booklet that contained an itinerary of her trip, a short list of the personal gear she would need, and a series of horse riding tips. In three weeks Shelby would fly to Boise, Idaho and take a four hour drive in an old green Ford work truck to the trail head. Shelby imagined the Ford smelled of dirty socks and unfermented manure.

Jackson reassured Shelby that she would enjoy the ride and with some patience, she would ultimately learn that this would be the best choice she could make. In anger she took off her oversized sunglasses, glared at her Mom, rolled her eyes and stormed out of the meeting room. She threw the colored booklet in the air as she left and it fluttered to the floor like a wounded gossamer-winged butterfly. Jackson grinned, as he knew this experience was exactly what Shelby needed.

"We all begin with our eyes closed, as we are before we are born." Jackson said to Joanne. Joanne knew by Jackson's tone it was not meant in a religious and controlling sense, but rather with spiritual and liberated significance, which troubled her. Joanne picked up the booklet as she left the room. Joanne was particularly angered by Shelby's indifference and disrespectful actions in the presence of both Jackson and Father Herrera.

3   A Clear Understanding

Show respect to all people, but grovel to none.
Tecumseh - Shawnee

1:47 was illuminated on the radio display panel as *Guns-N-Roses* blared out on tinny speakers in the rusted truck door. It was at this early morning hour that Curtis Moore left his bartending job at the local dive, The Velvet Cushion. Every western small town has at least one of these smoky, oppressive watering holes. It was the kind of establishment where the karaoke microphone smells of stale Coors, and the divorced clientele outnumber the flies in the greasy kitchen. But that's the *new* American west - struggles, contention, and arrogant self-expression at every turn.

Curtis, or Curt as his father called him, always wanted more with his life than to stay in his dreary hometown after high school. Instead, Curt put life off and rarely strayed from Ode, Montana. Curt and a couple of old friends had a tendency to drink too much on Thursday, Friday and Saturday nights. They either started fights or managed to end up, somehow, up river in the town of Silver. Too drunk to drive, they more often than not spent the night in the town's foul-smelling holding cell. It was one of these garish nights out with the boys when they decided to go to the Fireside Cocktail Lounge. It was another fine establishment of debauchery and ill repute where *drunk* is a noun, a verb and frequently a state of mind. On this particular second-rate night of drinking, Curt had broken on a game of nine-ball billiards when he noticed a woman about his age walk through the bar, alone. She was dressed in tight jeans, an oversized denim jacket but was significantly better looking than most women that crossed the threshold of this derelict lounge. Curt halfway recognized her. He hadn't seen…oh-what's-her-name, what felt like a decade, but was realistically closer to six years. He continued to play his game and peered over his shoulder to find out if Sheena, Shelly, no, Susan, yeah, that was it, Susan, was alone or with another guy. After he had discreetly snuck several lecherous glances over at her, trying to remember her name, he was convinced, it wasn't Susan. Jennifer? No, that wasn't it either. He played on. Curt was distracted and near the end of this losing game. With his back towards the bar he mulled over his next shot. Curt was then lightly tapped on the shoulder. He turned, expecting his buddy Steve Parker to be screwing with him, but it was Shelby.

"Aren't you Curtis Moore?" Shelby asked as she smiled and took a small swig of her half empty bottle of Bud Light.

"Ya-Yep." Curt stuttered as he was taken by surprise.

"Don't you remember me? Back in high school we had math together with Mr. Erickson. But I think you were a year ahead of me. Remember, algebra?" Then her name came to him.

"Shelby Gilbert, right?" Curt asked.

"Garrett" she quickly replied, "Shelby Garrett."

"I thought I recognized you when you came in, but wasn't sure it was you. It's been a few years and well I don't keep in touch with people from back then." Curt said.

"Ain't-cha gonna' introduce me to your purddy friend there Curt ol' bud?" It was his good ol' buddy Steve Parker who had stepped in to the conversation speaking in his finest drunken stammer.

"Back-off Steve. This is Shelby Garrett. Remember her from school?" Curt was clearly annoyed at Steve's inebriated demeanor.

"Oh-how could I fer-get your sweet little smile?" Steve boorishly raked his eyes down her body to end ogling her butt.

"You're still a pig Steve, only older and uglier!" Shelby replied. "I won't be seeing you Steve, but I'll see you around Curtis." Shelby slammed down her bottle of beer on the table and walked out without waiting for a reply from either Curt or Steve. The bar was silent with all eyes on the swinging door as Shelby left. The beer bottle rattled to a deafening stop.

"You truly are an ass, man." Curt snapped at Steve. Curt shook his head in disbelief at what had happened and figured he wouldn't be seeing Shelby again. Steve gave Curt a pathetic *what did I do* look. Too bad, Curt thought. Shelby was always pretty friendly back in high school and gave him the impression she was much nicer now. He continued and eventually lost his nine-ball game. Without saying another word to Steve, Curt mumbled to himself. 'Hmm, Shelby Garrett, imagine that.'

At nearly eleven the following morning, Curt was down at the self-serve carwash, giving his truck an overdue cleaning. He couldn't remember the last time he had washed or cleaned out his rusted, two-tone truck. He was nearly finished in the wash bay, when up drove a new carbon-silver Cadillac. It was not the big four-door model, but the edgy coupe with tinted windows and flashy chrome wheels. Curt noticed the driver, an older man, but completely overlooked the woman passenger. He didn't take time to recognize who they were. He finished washing and rinsing and without another thought, jumped in his truck and drove it out of the wash bay and to the vacuum station. Curt dug into his jeans to retrieve four quarters to dump into the stainless steel canister vacuum. Out of the corner of his eye he noticed someone as they approached and he looked up.

It was the man from the carbon-silver Caddy and to his surprise, Shelby Garret

"Hey Curtis." Shelby called out with a radiant smile.

"Hi." He said and smiled back. Curt removed his hand from his pocket and two quarters tumbled on the ground. He nodded to the man who was with Shelby to acknowledge him.

"Dad," Shelby politely said, "this is Curtis. We went to school together. Do you remember him?"

"I don't think I do?" Shelby's Dad said as he extended his hand to Curt and scrutinized this old friend of his only daughter.

"Curt Moore." Curt shyly said, as they shook hands.

"Oh, it's Curt now huh?" Shelby smirked. "Well, this is my Dad, James. We thought we'd come and introduce him and invite you over to a barbeque this afternoon. It's Daddy's birthday."

"Well happy birthday, Mr. Garrett." Curt said, as he smiled at Shelby. "It would be great to catch up with you, Shelby. What time should I come by?"

"Say between 5:30 and 6:00 – it's at 454 Spruce View Drive. You know, back behind the golf course." Shelby replied.

"Great!" Curt said. Curt nervously jingled the remaining two quarters in his hand.

"Well, I'd better get the ol' gal washed." Mr. Garrett said. He paused and again extended his hand out to Curt. "And it was good meeting you, Curt. I guess I'll be seeing you this evening." Mr. Garrett turned and walked back to the wash bay. Curt and Shelby talked until Mr. Garrett finished washing his Caddy and pulled up to the vacuum station, where he waved-in Shelby with a turn of his head. Curt and Shelby smiled as they waved good-bye. Curt got in his truck and drove off thinking of Shelby, forgetting about the vacuum and spilled coins.

It was 5:47 p.m. when Curt drove up to the Garrett home to find a street full of cars and several people parking as he was. He parked three houses down, on the same side of the street as the Garrett residence. With nervous anticipation, Curt walked up to the house. To his pleasant surprise, Shelby was waiting for him near the front door as she talked with a woman who Curt presumed could be a relative. Curt approached and slowed his pace to let Shelby recognize him. He didn't know Shelby had been watching inconspicuously from the living room window. Shelby conveniently walked outside to meet him after Curt drove by.

Shelby took Curt on a short round of introductions, small talk with a few guests, and again with Mr. Garrett, who now insisted on being called James. This seemed awkward to Curt, but he acquiesced. After a few more introductions, Curt and Shelby retreated to the deck. She told him how her mom took her to a ridiculous church seminar and signed her up for this crazy wilderness life journey in Oregon.

"Can you believe it Curt? Would your mom sign you up to head out to the wilderness with god-knows-who to do god-knows-what? To top it off, she expects me to be grateful for it?" She continued with a single breath. "And to make matters worse, I'll have to miss my favorite soap, for two weeks!" She paused. "Then to top that, they expect *me* to ride a horse, sleep in a tent, and NO TV and no shower! What in the hell was she thinking?" A look of pure exasperation came over Shelby's face. She fully expected to get a healthy dose of sympathy from Curt.

"Sounds fun." Curt said without missing a beat.

"What? Fun? What's *wrong* with you?" Shelby glared. He felt the deep indignation his words caused her.

"Can you really picture me out there? I don't do *the woods*. What makes you think it would be fun? What do you know about the horses and sleeping in tents?" Shelby questioned, irritated by Curt's lack of consideration.

"Well," Curt started hesitantly, "if it were me, I'd be looking forward to getting out of *this* town, seeing a part of the world I've never been to and maybe even meeting new people." He continued as she looked at him in disbelief. "It might be good to be a cowboy for a while without having to buy the whole ranch."

"So you really think it would be a whole bunch of fun to play cowboy? You would skip the bars and partying with your buddies for a whole bunch of spiritual mountain bullshit?" She paused, looked him in the eyes and continued. "You really don't understand me do you? No one does, and that's why mom is sending me off to this holy-roller adventure crap." Curt stood in stunned silence for a mere second.

"You're right Shelby. I don't understand or really know you. Back in high school, you were fun to be around and you were always a nice person. I know that if I had the chance to get the hell out of this ass-backward town, even for a week, and someone that cared enough for me to help me get there, well, I guess I wouldn't be so unhappy about it." She stared at him. Curt continued. "You know, maybe this trip to the woods is not your kind of fun, but trying is part of the adventure. And you like to have a good time, don't you?"

Shelby was about to speak, then paused, thought about what he had said.

"If you think this trip would be so much fun, why don't you come along? It's only, like, twenty five hundred dollars. You can leave your lousy bar hopping fun to your buddy, what's-his-face, Pig or whatever his name is. Should I have my mom sign you up too?" She stared madly, waiting for him to say no, solely to prove she would be right. Curt stared back at her as he deliberated his rebuttal. Shifted his body nervously and finally blurted out.

"Okay. Okay. If I can figure a way to get that much money and maybe, just maybe Ramona, my boss, will let me take some time off, I'll go." Shelby was stunned.

"You'll drop everything, maybe lose your job and go with me to do this spiritual woods thing?" Shelby said in questioning disbelief.

"If I can get the money, I'll go." Curt quickly replied. Knowing it would be next to impossible for him to come up with that sum of money in short order. He thought this was his out. Shelby stared in thought for a moment, instinctually knowing he would weasel out if given the chance because that's what guys have always done to her. Promise, promise, promise and leave her hanging, alone. She promptly took out her shimmering, rhinestone clad cell phone from her pants pocket.

"So what's the number to your work so you can ask for time off?" She asked. Curt agreeably took the phone from Shelby's French manicured hand, dialed the bar's phone number, waited, then spoke into the phone.

"Hey Mandy, this is Curt. Is Ramona in?" There was a pause in the conversation as Mandy went to find Ramona.

"So when are we going?" Curt asked Shelby, while he waited for Ramona.

"Leaving July 31st and we'll be back in about two weeks." Shelby replied.

"Two weeks? I can't be gone for two weeks, its summer and..." Ramona came on the line.

"Hey Ramona, this is Curt. I was hoping to take two weeks off starting on the 31st so I figured I'd give you a call and see...." There was a pause, and Curt spoke again. "No, not of August, of July." Shelby could hear Ramona's raised voice as Curt inched the phone away from his ear, still listening as he winced.

"Well, if I can get Mandy to cover my shifts and her sister Pam can cover her shifts, will that work?" Curt asked. Again, the cringe on Curt's face returned, then slowly subsided. There was another long pause on the phone. "Hi, Mandy do you think you can cover my shifts for two weeks starting on July 31st?" Again, the phone retreated from his ear and a short smile grew on his face. "Yes. Yes. I know I'll owe you one Mandy. I promise I'll make good on this, you'll see. I won't let you down." He pleaded to Mandy then ended their conversation. "Now, where am I going to get the money to pay for this trip?" He rhetorically commented.

"Not to worry. Mom will gladly pay your part in exchange for me not bitching about this trip anymore. Not only that, you can't get out of this trip-to-Dante's hell either." Shelby said in a self-serving tone she was known for and was so, so good at. Curt ignorantly smiled back and thought. 'What did I get myself into?' He walked to the beer cooler setting on the sun deck. Grabbed a beer and was about to get a second for Shelby and said. "Care for a cold Bud…" He realized Shelby was gone. Curt was left on the deck with only his thoughts and a beer in hand. He closed the lid of the beer cooler and plopped himself down astonished at what had happened. He barely knew Shelby and he had agreed to head off to camping in wild Oregon. Maybe she won't get her mom to pony up the cash. Curt thought. Maybe Mandy or Ramona would change their mind. Curt ran through the possibilities of what could or would go wrong. Regardless, he would remain jammed in this dead end town.

Curt sat on the cooler as he drank his beer and wondered what Shelby was up to. Would she figure a way to get him to go on this trip or was this his way out of the situation he foolishly got himself into. As he considered the possible outcomes, Shelby had pulled Joanne and James away from their guests and into the confines of Mr. Garrett's office to plead her case.

"Mom, now you know I don't want to go to this wilderness trip. It was your idea and you took me unwillingly to that seminar at your church!"

"Our church. Not my church. Our church." Joanne pointed her finger to Shelby and James and back to herself.

"Okay, okay, our church." Shelby agreed with mild disapproval. "Here is the deal. I'll go on this miserable trip," she paused, rolled her eyes, and then continued, "if you would please let me go with Curt."

"Well I don't know about this Shelby, he seems like kind of a good-for-nothing. He drives that old beat up rusty truck and doesn't seem like the most respectable kind. What will people think?" James immediately stated.

"What about what I think? I think I'm being sent to this no-where land with no one I know and it is going to be horrible. That is what I think, but you obviously don't care about what I think!" Again eyes rolling, Shelby retorted in the best bitchy-whiney-sniveling voice she could muster.

"Alright Shelby!" Joanne stepped in, holding her hand to the height of Shelby's mouth. "If he goes, how do you know we can trust him?" Again, pointing with her finger at James, Shelby and herself. "What if he takes advantage?"

"Advantage of me? Please! Mom, Dad, you know me better. There is no one that takes advantage of ME! Anyway, he'll owe us."

"What do you mean, owe us?" James demanded.

"Well," Shelby paused, "I told Curt you would pay for his trip if he agreed to go. In return, Mommy, Daddy, I promise, promise, promise not to complain about this trip, not even once. I really promise." Joanne and James both looked at one another in disbelief and anticipation. Both instinctually thought no complaints, no attitude, and no further problems about this trip for a whole three weeks. That had its price in itself.

"Well, alright. But I need to have a talk with this boy. Myself. You know, man-to-man." James said. Joanne stood in silence shaking her head in confused agreement.

"Okay, okay, okay! I love you." Shelby said in earnest as she gave both parents a short but meaningful hug. "I'll go get him!"

"No, no. I'll go have a word with him. I suppose he's out drinking MY beer. I'll find him and you," James stated, as he pointed his finger to Joanne, "you need to have a talk with her about you know what." James turned and left the office. I was right. James thought to himself. Drinking MY beer, on MY deck. Damn low-life!

"Curt!" James announced his arrival as he exited the French doors leading to the expansive sun deck. Curt stood and found himself with Mr. Garrett while the rest of the friends and relatives were inside, shielding themselves from the hot afternoon sun. James continued. "I understand you want to go with my daughter on the wilderness trip and you're expecting us to cover expenses for you."

"Mr. Garrett, Sir." Curt said. "Shelby asked what I thought about the trip and I honestly told her I thought it would be a good thing. She somehow managed to convince me I should go along and insisted her mom would cover the cost. I want to go, but I honestly don't think I can come up with the $2,500 needed in three weeks, Sir."

"Shelby does have a way of getting what she wants, doesn't she." James concluded rhetorically. Then he pondered the situation for an instant and said to Curt. "If you do go along, how do I know I can trust you with my daughter?" James glared into Curt's eyes and moved uncomfortably close to him.

"Mr. Garrett, I really believe there is no one you can trust with your daughter more than me. Anyway, I don't think anyone can take advantage of her, even if they wanted to." At that moment, there was a gleam of immense satisfaction in James' eyes, knowing that Curt understood his daughter's fortitude in the same light as he did.

"True. Too true." James said with a confident grin. Before he turned and walked back into his guest filled home, James leaned in towards Curt with an extended hand. He grabbed Curt's right hand with an iron tight grip. He drew Curt in closer. He looked sternly in his eyes and spoke slowly and softly. "I'm typically not a man of violence, but believe me," and after a death-long pause, "if you hurt my Shelby, in any way, I'll rip out your blue eyes and leave you blind and crippled. Am I clear,... Mr. Moore?"

"Of - of course, Sir." Curt managed to stammer in stunned fear.

Without emotion, James walked back to his waiting guests. With a sudden big grin, he greeted a guest as if nothing had been said outside to the now bewildered Curt.

Moments later Shelby rushed out of the house with a smile a mile wide.

"How did you convince him, Curt?" Shelby said as she rushed to Curt and gave him an enthusiastic hug.

"Convince him? I think his mind was made before he ever stepped out here. I think he wanted to make his position clear, is all." Curt replied. Shelby understood her dad all too well and read Curt's fearful expression with no explanation needed.

4 Two Spirit Worlds

Our nation was born in genocide when it embraced the doctrine that the original American, the Indian, was an inferior race. Even before there were a large number of Negroes on our shore, the scar of racial hatred had already disfigured colonial society. From the sixteenth century forward, blood flowed in battles over racial supremacy. We are perhaps the only nation which tried as a matter of national policy to wipe out its indigenous population. Moreover, we elevated that tragic experience into a noble crusade. Our literature, our films, our drama, our folklore all exalt it. Our children are still taught to respect the violence which reduced a red-skinned people of an earlier culture to a few fragmented groups herded into impoverished reservations.
John F. Kennedy

The sun beat down fiercely on this mid-summer morning. It was nearly eleven, and the heat reflected off the sandy trail that led to the burial grounds of Father Ricardo Fernando de Herrera's ancestors. As he neared the sacred grounds of his departed father and mother, he sweltered beneath the cloudless sky. Every footfall was heavier than the previous. He had been walking now for five hours and felt anxious to arrive. Throughout his pilgrimage he prayed to God and his ancestors to find the wisdom and direction he desperately sought.

There was no shade as he staggered on. The trail he followed would disappear, reappear then fade again. He followed his instincts, listened to the winds and followed the nearly indistinguishable signs of the trail that led him to an elongated rocky plateau. At the eastern edge of the sandstone outcrop were several rock burial mounds. The outcrop was sparsely vegetated with short rabbit brush and blue gramma grass, and was the final resting place of his ancestors. He passed the first then second burial mound. As he approached the third burial mound he collapsed onto his knees. His dusty hands reached forward as he slumped. Father Herrera grasped the exposed lichen crusted sandstone of the burial mound. Tears trickled from his sad eyes, brightening the sea green lichen as they fell on to the sandstone. He no longer felt the hot sun nor the long passage. He wept in inconsolable sorrow.

Father Ricardo Fernando de Herrera, was a troubled soul. Born the only son of a Jicarilla Apache family and raised after his tenth year by his distant, and strictly Catholic, uncle and aunt. He was sent to live with them after his father, mother, and younger sister were stricken with a rare influenza and all passed away. He felt he had no one and this emptiness burdened him. His uncle and aunt had left the reservation many years before this tragedy. They took him back to live with them in a small village in the mountains, far from his native land, and into a life of strict Catholicism. As a young boy, he was required to attend mass every morning just after dawn and both morning and afternoon services on Sundays. The church centered his every moment, conversation and family life. Decisions and discussions were based on the perception and how they affected The Church. He was torn between the natural instincts of his Native American culture and the disciplined ways of the church. He always knew he was born to serve his people through his faith. His passion for caring and helping those in need of guidance and spiritual enlightenment was ingrained into this man of the cloth. After many years of serving the church, he felt there was no other way. Although he believed in Catholicism, it was with an aura of perplexing reluctance. He stayed atop the rocky mesa on his knees, praying for hours at the gravesite of his father.

    With the light of morning he awoke. He felt he was being watched. But there was no one in this isolated area of the southwest. He wiped the sleep from his eyes. His dream from the night abruptly came to him. It was a white spider spinning a single silken webbed line from a distant bright hole above. He reached above his head with his right hand for the shimmering silver web. As he held it, he grew lighter. Now weightless, the light above grew brighter. He abruptly awoke to the cool early morning air. But was it a dream? Or was it real? Was this unwittingly the spiritual guidance he had come to find? The thoughts and visions of his dream ran through his mind repeatedly. This dream confused him the more he thought about it. What did this dream mean? Did it mean anything at all? He stood and looked to the rising sun and hoped for clarity and true understanding. Again, he fell to his knees, grasped the sparsely lichen-covered sandstone of the burial mound and prayed for direction. No guiding wisdom came.

After three more hours of prayer, he painstakingly stood, raised both hands to the warm blue sky and again saw the shimmering web beyond the tips of his fingers. The end of the web descended, very slowly. Once it had lowered far enough for him to grasp, the web swiftly wrapped itself around his hand. Again he became weightless and ascended for a mere instant then fell oppressively to the hard earth. Seeking understanding, he again rose. He stood arms stretched to the heavens but no guiding wisdom came. His arms lowered in crushing despair as he stood in silence in the morbid stillness of the morning. There were no song birds; no chatter of insects, only a large dark raptor could be seen gliding in the rising thermals. He began his arduous walk out of this spiritual land of his ancestors. Father Herrera saw himself as a solitary man walking between two spirit worlds. He was persecuted between the deep rooted pillars of Catholicism and the ghost winds of his native soul.

5   The Cross

The real danger is the gradual erosion of individual liberties through automation, integration, and interconnection of many small, separate record-keeping systems, each of which alone may seem innocuous, even benevolent, and wholly justifiable.
US Privacy Study Commission

Katherine Roberts, CIA Officer #49387, a native of Roanoke, Virginia, and the daughter of retired CIA Director of the Office of Terrorism Analysis, stood at the window of her Quantico office. Officer Roberts, or as her father called her, Katy, was sharply dressed in her finest charcoal designer business attire. She was in her ninth year of service with The Company. Her experience and position as one of the up and coming Terrorism Analysts, she commanded a distinct level of well-earned respect amongst her colleagues. Katy's warm and welcoming demeanor suited her well. She used this to her advantage in getting information and insight The Company sought from the worst criminals and terrorism organizations.

Staring out her window, she watched a gray-haired man in a blue workman's uniform mow the extensive and lush greenscape that surrounded her building. Patiently moving in a circling pattern, much the way a predator will watch, circle and slowly close in on its prey. As she watched, she thought of the similarity of the lawnmower man below and her current case. She and her team of analysts were trying to close in on the threatening person or organization who had been sending conical shaped rifled musket bullets to two prominent female Senators and a Congressman from New York. This was a warning the Office of Terrorism Analysis took very seriously.

The bullets consisted of a single handmade .50 caliber round which were conical with horizontal grooves. Each was antique with a patina only time could bring. What really caught the attention of the CIA was not so much their uniqueness, but rather where they had been discovered. The first was found in the top drawer of a jewelry cabinet in the bathroom of Senator M.C. Phillips' home in the upper East end of Manhattan. The bullet was neatly placed where her mother's emerald ring was always kept. The emerald ring had been removed. The bullet was placed between the velvet ring cushions then the ring was then replaced around the pointed end of this deadly round.

The second bullet was similarly placed at the vacation home of Senator Claire Holden in Hampton

Bay. The third rifled bullet was found on the oil on canvas portrait of Congressman George C. Cussler. The bullet was held on the canvas with spines of cholla cactus, placing the round centered on his forehead. The three rounds certainly caught the attention of these well known Senators and Congressman, but more importantly, brought the attention of the top brass at the CIA. This unusual case was classified as top priority and full staffing to Officer Katy Robert's team was approved. She pondered the case in silence. Her thoughts were interrupted by a harsh and rapid knock at her door. She turned at the jolt then coolly replied.

"Come in." As if nothing ever rattled her. Officer Gary Nelson entered the room in alarm. This was just the beginning of this priority case.

"What do you have Nelson?" Katy quickly asked. Without saying a word, he handed her the latest photos of a newly reported rifled musket bullet. The photos showed another .50 caliber round, the fourth, placed neatly in a Victorian styled pewter jewelry box kept on the night stand at the home of the U.S. Secretary of State, Margaret A. Vance. The photo was taken shortly after she had arrived back from a state dinner with the president and the prime ministers of both China and India.

The Secretary of State was aware of the previous threats to the New York senators and congressman through her daily national security briefing, but this chilled her. The round must have been placed earlier today after she left for her state dinner. The bullet was placed where she kept her mother's antique platinum and sapphire ring that she wore to dinner. She reported leaving her bedroom, after a brief respite, at 6:01p.m when her car arrived. The photos were taken at 11:09 p.m. an hour after her return. Each photo had a red numbered date stamp of 23:09 on the bottom right corner. There was nothing special in the first photo, simply a shot of the entrance into the bedroom, and the second an equally unimpressive shot of a closed and locked exterior door. It was the third photo in the short stack which caught Katy's attention. The photo showed a full shot of the headboard, white ruffled edged pillows, nightstand with a jewelry box where the round was located and the upper half of the bed. On the left hand side of the photo, on the nightstand, a white lace doily was turned up. On the doily was the Secretary's digital alarm clock. It was as if the doily was purposely dog-eared.

"Which side of the bed does the Secretary sleep on?" Katy demanded of Nelson.

"I'll find out. What do you see?" Nelson nervously asked as if he should have noticed anything that was amiss in the photos before he brought them in to Officer Roberts, his Controller.

"Well, maybe nothing, maybe something." Katy pointed to the dog eared doily, while she looked at Nelson.

"I'll have the uniformed officers on-site have a closer look and I'll get back with you." Nelson replied. As he left the room, he was calling the on-scene officer, leaving Katy to study the photos. Not three minutes passed when Nelson blew in to Katy's office, barely knocking and opening the door without waiting for a reply. He showed her a new photo of the dog-eared doily beneath the alarm clock. Placed on the doily was a small, flat, alabaster Christian cross.

The cross appeared to be no more than three inches tall and slightly over an inch wide and less than a tenth of an inch thick. Thin and small enough to sit unnoticed beneath the alarm clock. The next photo showed the back side of the cross. Engraved at its center appeared to be a small dog with a bushy tail. The long, upright portion of the cross was etched with a stout four legged animal that had short legs and a wide head.

"Any idea what the symbols represent?" Katy asked Nelson.

"Not yet. I sent photos to Cultural Resources and they will be working on this as soon as they receive the cross." Nelson replied.

"What about the others? Has anything similar been found at their locations?" Katy quickly asked.

"No reports of anything out of the ordinary, but maybe they weren't looking close enough." Nelson shot back.

"Have them look again and be sure they see this cross and where it was found." Katy said as she handed back the stack of photos, keeping only the one photo with the bushy tailed dog and stout animal.

The remainder of the morning passed without news. It was a routine day of following up on leads, reviewing lab results, phone calls and attending rescheduled meeting. On Katy's schedule was a mandatory seminar on *Theoretical Computer Applications in Psychological Profiling,* which was to be held in Atlanta, Georgia in two weeks.

This new threat to Secretary Vance would definitely be her one-way ticket out of this two-day geek-fest, Katy thought. No sooner did she begin to delete the seminar from her schedule when the phone rang. She paused, picked up the phone, stared at her calendar on the computer monitor, as if looking through it.

"They found the very same Christian cross at two of the three locations. They both had the same placement, beneath the bedside alarm clock. They also found out that each of the alarms had been set to 5:03 p.m., including the alarm clock at the Secretary of State's home. Oddly, the alarm of Senator Claire Holden was set to 5:03 *a.m.* They were still searching at Congressman George C. Cussler's home at last report." Nelson stated. Katy cautiously processed this new information, told Nelson thanks and to keep her informed. She continued to stare through the monitor.

"Same round, same cross, same times, two senators, a congressman from the same state and Secretary Vance. But Vance was from D.C.?" Katy spoke out loud. What or who am I missing? She thought to herself. She continued running the details of what she knew of the case information through her head. She picked up the phone, pressed speed-dial number seven that rang to Nelson.

"Nelson." Katy heard on the other end.

"Has the mode of entry or any prints been identified at any of the .50 caliber locations?" Katy asked as she now stared with intrigue at the lawnmower man below.

"That's what has the teams puzzled. At each location, the alarm system was on and there was no evidence that anyone entered the homes. No prints, zero. In Senator M.C. Phillips' home there is a surveillance system that showed no interruption and no entry. There was no surveillance camera in the Hampton Bay home bedroom but the security system is top notch and didn't identify any down time or alarm. As far as Secretary Vance's home, her daughter and granddaughter were at her residence the entire evening and neither heard nor saw anything. The security system was on, and there was no evidence of anyone leaving the home after the Secretary left for her dinner and certainly no one entering until her return. Still no word from Cultural Resources and no cross has been located at Senator Cussler's home." Nelson reported to Katy.

"Not yet, anyway." Katy retorted.

As Katy pressed the hands-free phone button to end the call, she continued to study the successive circular pattern the lawnmower man had created. She wondered who would be found at the epicenter of these mysterious threats.

6 Old Bones

Laws are spider webs through which the big flies pass and the little ones get caught.
Honore de Balzac – French novelist and playwright

At five-fifteen a.m. near Quantico, Virginia, a yellow cab arrived slightly ahead of schedule to an upscale Victorian home, surrounded by majestic Pin Oaks. The cabby stepped out into the drizzle and pre-dawn light. He lifted Officer Katy Roberts' stuffed black suitcase and night bag into the trunk of the cab. Katy slipped into the passenger side rear seat with briefcase in hand. The yellow cab slowly pulled around the cobblestone circular driveway, onto Cardinal Drive. It continued past the Montclair Country Club and onto I-95 towards Quantico Marine Corps Base where the jet and pilot awaited her arrival. Katy arrived at Quantico well before traffic was heavy. She paid the cabbie the customary $50 fare, including tip.

"See you when you return, Ms. Roberts." The cabby said. He gladly took the folded $50 bill with a thanking smile.

Katy stepped into the cabin of the richly appointed jet. In the third row waited Mark Kelley,

Director of the CIA Office of Terrorism Analysis. He was a gray bearded man in his mid fifties who looked ten years older. He read the night's analysis updates with a disgruntled look on his face. Katy sat in the seat across the aisle and placed her briefcase on her lap. Mark slid the report onto her briefcase.

"Seems to me you need to call Cultural Resources and get the whole story on the crosses. It appears they are struggling with this one." Mark greeted Katy.

"And good morning to you, Sir." Katy replied as she picked up the update and began to scan the page to find out what Cultural Resources reported:

```
Case #87351(Roberts) Cultural
Resources determination
uncertain of origin of white
cross symbolism, origin or
significance. Preliminary
report etching #1 on reverse
location is possibly a dog,
wolf or coyote. Etching #2 on
reverse location is
potentially an insect, bird or
lizard. END.
```

"Bird? Insect? Bull-shit!" Katy snapped angrily. She unlocked her cell phone; pressed speed dial 11 and after only one ring she sternly asked the

Cultural Resource person. "Bird? Insect? Please explain to me what kind evidence you have that shows a four-legged animal as a bird or insect? I need to know what these symbols mean and what they are doing on the white cross and what relationship they have with the cross and the .50 caliber rounds they were found with!" There was a slight pause as she listened to a rattled Cultural Resource Staff's reply.

"I need accurate, realistic, and well researched answers! Now, help me to the bottom of this. I'll be expecting a reliable report by the time I leave Atlanta in two days." Katy ended her phone call. She cast the worthless report on to the empty seat next to her.

"Good news." Nelson said as he stepped in to the cabin of the jet. He took the seat behind Director Kelly, bent forward to overcome the rising engine noise. "Not five minutes ago the Field Analysts found a third cross at Congressman George Cussler's home, but it was different."

"How is this good news?" Director Kelly asked Nelson. "Those damn Senators want answers and are making a real stink!"

"Different how?" Katy asked.

"Good evidence Director, plus the cross was made from the same material, bone, but the shape was similar to a swastika and the symbols were clearly of a man and a spider." Nelson reported. "The cross was taken to Cultural Resources for analysis and we should hear back later today."

"Don't count on it, did you read the case updates?" Katy asked Nelson, as she handed the report to him.

"Bird? They called that lizard-like etching on the first cross a damn bird? So much for expecting credible information from Cultural Resources." Nelson replied.

"Katy, you need to consider a way to get some field time where you can directly investigate what these symbolic crosses mean. While Cultural Resources can do quite a bit for you, on the ground work may be your best option to get answers for me and the men and women on the hill. It's likely not going to be easy to find access, but it takes creative approach to answer the difficult questions. Get my point?"

"Yes Director Kelly, I'll work out a solution. The theoretical seminar may give me an opportunity to talk to some research people and network with others that may have a fresh approach. Good thinking."

Director Kelly nodded his head in agreement with Katy's plan.

As the jet taxied towards the runway, Katy was deep in thought with her head resting back, and her eyes closed. Katy knew whom to call. She dialed The Company operator.

"Good morning Liz. Could I please get the number to our Native American liaison in Portland, Oregon? I believe his name is Ian or Ira." There was an expected pause as the operator looked for the information. Katy then wrote: *503-569-8787, Ira K.* She dialed the number, expecting to get an answering machine as Oregon was three hours behind and they wouldn't quite be out of bed. When the answering machine finished the pre-recorded message Katy left a message for Officer Knight: "Officer Knight, this is Officer Roberts from HQ. We met last year in Oklahoma. I have a burning priority case and I was hoping to get your insight. Please call me as soon as possible at 202-689-9635. Thank you Ira." She closed the call and her eyes at the same instant. The remainder of the flight to Atlanta was pleasantly quiet.

The plane touched down on a secondary runway at Hartsfield-Jackson Atlanta International and taxied to the waiting black Chevy SUV. The three Officers had their luggage loaded into the vehicle by the driver. They got in and drove off to the Southeast Federal Facility for their seminar on Theoretical Computer Applications in Psychological

Profiling. It was going to be a long, long two days, Katy thought.

They arrived at their seminar and during their first morning break, there was a message on Katy's phone. It was from Ira in Portland. She promptly returned his call.

"Officer Knight." Ira answered.

"Officer Knight, this is Officer Katy Roberts, thank you for returning my call so quickly. I'm so sorry I was not available when you called. If you have a moment, I would appreciate your help on our case. I believe you may be able to help us move it forward." Katy asked.

"Sure thing Officer Roberts, how can I help?" Ira replied.

"This is our situation. We found four small bone crosses, one shaped similar to a swastika and three others like a Christian cross. The swastika cross has etchings of a man and a spider. While the Christian crosses all have the same dog or coyote etching in the center plus a lizard-looking animal on the back side. Cultural Resources have researched them, but are having a challenge with the symbolism. Any immediate thoughts? There was the expected pause as Ira envisioned the details.

"Have the images and any forensic details sent to me, I'll look at them. I'll call you back once I have a chance to study and research them." Ira replied.

"They were sent to you half-hour ago via your encrypted D-server. Look for case #87351. I look forward to learning what you think. And by the way, it's Katy."

Three hours passed and Katy had grown tired of the theoretical applications lecture. Between the conceptual and theoretical presentations she was getting antsy. She then noticed as Nelson exited the back of the conference room at a quick pace. Katy recognized his familiar hurried gait when information was hot. She quietly excused herself from the room and found Nelson on the phone. He wrote furiously, listened, and then wrote again. She walked up to him and read through his abbreviations: *Swstka - man-life / spdr-unk. Cross - coyote/gila mstr. Fear/trks/drms.* Nelson was on the phone for a minute more when he again scrawled: *bone-human, 5K?* Nelson finished, said a customary thank you and ended his phone call.

"That was Cultural Resources. The bone is possibly human and all four crosses are likely more than 5,000 years old. They are processing the age of the crosses, but need more time to get the results. The swastika shaped cross with the etching of the man means life, but they still don't understand the significance of the spider. They are still working on that one. On the other three crosses, the dog etching is really a coyote, that supposedly means fear and trickery and the lizard looking etching is what is known as a Gila monster, which is a symbol for dreams or dreaming." Nelson reported. Both Nelson and Katy struggled with this new information and had many more questions that needed further analysis.

"Anything else? What do they mean in context to one another?" Katy asked.

"No report at this time. They'll be calling with more information as they gather answers." Nelson finished. They both returned to their seats, mulling over the bewildering and incomplete Cultural Resources informational report: Old human bones. Katy repeatedly studied Nelson's cryptic notes as she half-heartedly listened to the lengthy monotone lecture. It was 1:31 p.m. when Katy's phone silently buzzed. A call was coming from area code 503. It was Ira.

The afternoon session focused on several of the theoretical details of computer programming and their real life applications. Katy found the real applications fascinating, but questioned if their software program would work on an actual case.

Later the same evening, a much welcomed social hour was held at the pub in the adjacent hotel.

Katy listened to the live southern blues and jazz while she talked to a presenter, Dr. Michael Ku. He described in further detail some of the program's potential.

"Has it demonstrated viability in an actual case with real subjects, real questions and real information?" Katy asked, and then continued with her questioning. "Has it ever solved the type of social, cultural and psychological informational challenges we face at The Company?" She expected a roundabout answer that ended in no or never quite getting to the truth of the science of the applied theory. Dr. Ku then surprised Katy by skipping the bush beating and answered her.

"Yes, fully functional – occasional glitches, but multi-dimensional input capable."

"We'll see how it works when it gets to The Company, Dr. Ku." Katy smiled warmly even though she didn't believe his answer.

When the band finished their first set, Katy retreated to refresh her near empty drink at the bar. As Katy waited, up walked the band's singer, with a terracotta and white rimmed teacup in hand, gesturing to the bartender for a refill. The bartender nodded an affirmative reply.

"You're a stunning singer." Katy complimented the fashionably dressed blues singer.

She wore in a dazzling emerald sequined floor length evening gown. "Your last song, wasn't that Etta Jones? I remember that song from a long time ago when we lived in New York. My dad would listen to her and Houston Person."

"You know your jazz. And yes, you're right; Houston Person was her saxophonist for years. Leslie Jackson." Leslie reached out her hand to introduce herself after the flattering remark she received.

"Katherine Roberts, but my close friends call me Katy." They both politely shook hands and smiled at one another.

"Sissy," Leslie followed, "it's the name my grand-papa gave me when I was little because it just fit he said and Katy fits you quite pleasantly."

Sissy and Katy smiled at the friendly connection they instantly felt.

7   Cowboys and Peaceful Nights

Smell is a potent wizard that transports you across thousands of miles and all the years you have lived.
Helen Keller

Leslie Olivia "Sissy" Jackson was only seven years old when she first heard the sweet mournful melody of a single trumpet at the Savannah Music Festival. From that very moment, she knew she wanted to learn to play music that stirs the souls of the living and rattles the ashes of the dead. That sultry soft sound that somehow reaches into your very core, takes hold and no matter what you do, you know you just can't shake loose of it. It's always there, in the background of your thoughts like a soft Savannah rain.

At the age of ten Sissy performed at every southern fair she could get to. Played her hand-me-down horn that seemed to get silkier the more it was played. By age fourteen she was a very accomplished performer and sought after horn player for area festivals, celebrations and the occasional funeral as well. There was never a dry eye when the mournful cries of Sissy's southern gospel songs blessed the mourners. Several years later, Sissy finished her graduate degree from the University of Georgia's College of Music, when her mother unexpectedly died from an aortic aneurysm. This sudden event had a truly depressing and profound effect on Sissy's music. She moved back to Savannah, got a desk job with a small time CPA firm and relinquished her pursuit of music. For nearly two years, she played not a note. She had become distant from her family and kept clear of most friends. She occasionally went to Chatham Square where her momma would take her as a little girl. She would go there by herself and read an old book from her childhood for an hour or so and leave. Other times she would meet with her old school friend, have coffee or tea at the waterfront, and then quietly go home alone.

One particularly hot and oppressive afternoon after leaving the café, she was passing Parkers Bar, off East Washington Avenue. She stopped dead in her stride and listened to the same sad melody song that touched her nearly two decades before. Overcome by the texture and warmth of the atmosphere, with eyes closed, she listened. For the first time in so many months, she felt the once familiar grip on her heart and the rush in her soul that had left her. She listened for what seemed like an eternity but in truth was only a few minutes. She slowly walked off, humming to herself the soft, sweet, and comforting melody.

"What brings you to our fair Atlanta, Athens of the South, Katy?" Sissy asked in a southern drawl Katy found quite loveable.

"A long seminar on theoretical computer applications." She purposely left off, in psychological profiling. "It's sometimes cumbersome and tedious, but wonderful stuff, if it really works." Katy replied.

"I'm constantly on the road performing and always preparing for the next venue. It too is often cumbersome and tedious, and sounds like your work, Katy. I'm glad this weekend's big Atlanta Jazz Festival will be the last concert for a while." Sissy replied.

"Then what?" Katy pried with renewed interest.

"Now, this is quite out of character for me, but my family's pastor down in Savannah told me about this wilderness journey out west that brings you closer to nature. It gets me away from all this." Sissy replied, lightly gesturing at the crowd, commotion, and the stench of blue cigarette smoke that filled the room.

"Sounds like heaven." Katy said in agreement. "Where do I sign on? I can't imagine a weekend away from work and into the wild woods?"

"Week-end? Heavens no! This is no car ride through the country. It's two full weeks honey, plus travel time. Horses, cowboys and peaceful nights, yes peaceful nights. It's supposed to have a spiritual connection – you know, deep healing." Sissy replied.

"Two weeks? Horses? Where do you sleep?" Katy asked, amazed at the thought.

"Yeah horses. You sleep in a tent under the stars. The entire wilderness is a genuine ancient spiritual place. Like the way I said – a place for deep healing. We all need it from time to time." Sissy said. Katy recognized she was speaking from experience. There was hidden pain in this fabulous singer that she didn't let on to. Yet it was there. Like the deep luster of wood grain below the shine. Sissy took a long slow drink from her now steeped tea. She noticed the band getting back to the band stand.

"Gotta get back, honey. We can't keep Ella waitin'." She stood and walked off in her shimmering emerald gown, terracotta colored cup in hand. She seemed to glide across the edge of the hardwood dance floor to the bandstand. Katy smiled and waved lightly as Sissy walked off. Katy listened as Sissy and the band played Ella Fitzgerald's Honeysuckle Rose.

Eventually, Katy tired and found her way to her hotel room where she stewed over the crosses, symbols and the thoughts of getting away.

The seminar continued the following day with extended descriptions and application scenarios drawn out in detail – far too much detail, Katy thought. After eight and a-half grueling hours and to the point where the brain can no longer absorb more than the body can endure, the last session ended. Katy stepped out to an unwelcomed torrential rain storm. She again retreated to the little hotel pub were she had listened to soothing jazz the previous night. This evening however, there was no live music. A dreadful country crucifixion of an old Creedence Clearwater Revival song, *Have You Ever Seen the Rain* was being played on the karaoke machine. When she sat down, a voice came from behind her.

"May I join you?" It was Sissy.

"Oh, please do. I was having a bite before I head to my room. I was planning on heading back to Virginia tonight, but the plane was grounded." Katy replied, smiling at Sissy. Sissy sat and the waitress brought her a hot cup of water with a lemon wedge and a bag of herbal tea.

"So, Sissy, tell me more about your wilderness journey. You mentioned last night that you were visiting an ancient spiritual place out west and I'd like to learn more about it." Katy asked. She probed for information that might bring some more insight to her case.

"Really? You want to know about *my* trip to the woods?" Sissy replied in questioning disbelief.

"Yeah, it truly sounds fascinating." Katy replied with vital interest.

"Well, I've never been there, but the information on the booklet describes, let me think now. The entire area is supposed to be some ancient native sacred ground. There will be horseback riding, pristine alpine lakes, star gazing and wildlife viewing. Including elk, deer, eagles, coyotes, and wolves and moose..." Katy cut her off at mid sentence.

"Tell me more about coyotes? What did the booklet say about them?"

"Well, it only said we may see them, I think?" Sissy continued.

"What else did the booklet mention?" Katy pressed.

"We had to come prepared for bugs and spiders and peaceful dreams." That was all Katy needed to hear. This could potentially tie in with what Ira had told her when he called. He said that in ancient times there were beliefs that spiders would come into your dreams. The spider helped people understand, overcome fears, and brought healing. Conversely, the coyote was full of trickery, deceit, and brought chaos into your life. The symbol of the Gila Monster was also a representation of dreams. The etching of the man symbolized life. The crosses were the interesting part he had reported. The fact that one was in the shape of a swastika which was an ancient symbol representing the four directions of the wind, north, east, south and west. Objectively, it represented balance. The swastika symbol use by Native Americans preceded its distorted application by Nazi Germany by thousands of years. The fact that they were made of ancient bones could be the association with their human spirits. Unfortunately, this was only speculation as these symbols in association with each other and with the crosses had never been documented before. There were more questions to be answered in the two types of crosses and how they were found. Then, there were the .50 caliber rounds found at each site. They were meant to be found because of their placement in clear sight unlike the crosses, which were hidden. Katy felt there was a direct connection between the crosses and alarm clock time, but had no real evidence to support her speculation.

"Sissy, how would you like if I came along? We could be partners in this adventure. What do you say? I could stand for some real mind healing after this seminar." Katy said with diminished exuberance.

"Wow!" Sissy exclaimed, not expecting a new found friend in her life.

"Now are you really sure? It means really roughing it. There's more to you than I thought, Katy."

"You don't know the half of it Sissy" Katy answered. Katy told Sissy of her interest in the symbolic references of the animals and how it might help her case. Katy revealed nothing as to who was specifically involved. Katy astutely left out the potential international terrorism plots that were in progress and who might be behind them.

8   Yellow Eyed Dog

Sometimes one creates a dynamic impression by saying something, and sometimes one creates as significant an impression by remaining silent.
Dalai Lama – High Lama of Tibetan Buddhism

Everything was set for the trip. There had been six months of planning to get the right weeks scheduled for his solo wilderness adventure into the rugged peaks of the northwest's largest primitive area, the Eagle Cap Wilderness. Tom's backpack was full to capacity with only the finest hiking and camping supplies REI and North Face could offer. He would have fourteen days away from the monotonous board meetings, suits, long, drawn-out contracts and long days at Cooper & West Business Attorneys at Law. Tom Bade had managed to attain a lucrative counselor position with Cooper & West and needed the time to clear his mind from the everyday drudgery he found himself in. Tom's routine was up at five a.m., six days a week. Riding his Bianchi bike 13 miles to work through city traffic, then putting in 12-hour days and doing it again and again.

BLANKET OF DECEPTION

Tom had made it to work early on Monday. Sharply at nine a.m., as expected, into his office walked his assistant, Lisa Wyatt. In typical fashion, Tom didn't acknowledge her presence. He continued looking over the firm's latest profit and loss statement. She set onto his desk his daily opened and sorted stack of mail. She turned and proceeded out of his office.

"And where in the hell is my coffee?" Tom remarked without looking at Lisa. He rarely drank coffee. He purely insisted on being served.

"I'll be right back with it, sir." Lisa sprang back without looking at Tom. Lisa returned with coffee in hand and set it on the credenza. The coffee was left on the white marble coaster getting cold and never to be drunk.

"Will there be anything else?" Lisa asked. Tom didn't say a word and continued on with eyes fixed on the day's work. She left the office and as the door closed behind her she couldn't help but whisper, "Asshole."

"It's 10:35. Where in hell is my 10:30 appointment Lisa?" Tom's voice came over Lisa's telephone speaker.

Without missing a beat, she picked up the handset and courteously replied. "Mrs. Thomson will be right in. She is walking up the hall." There was no reply from Tom, just the closing click of the phone line. Typical, Lisa thought. When she showed Mrs. Thomson into his office, he grinned like a shark with ultra white teeth.

"Gina, right on time, please come in. Let's visit." Tom welcomed her, directing her to sit near him. Once again, as the door closed, Lisa whispered, "Asshole."

Not three minutes passed when Tom's voice came over Lisa's speakerphone.

"Lisa, dear, can you please bring in Mrs. Thomson's contract? We're now ready for it. Thanks." Lisa pulled the business contract she had prepared for Gina from the file, brought it in, gave Gina a courteous smile and again left without a word from Tom. The meeting lasted for 57 minutes and as Gina left Tom's office, she leaned over and whispered to Lisa.

"How do you stand to work for such a prick?" They both smiled and she walked off briskly. Tom noticed and disliked the brief exchange they enjoyed. Gina had left her business card discreetly on Lisa's desk. Picking it up to ensure it had been scanned into her file, she noticed the note on the backside of the elegant attorney's card: *Lisa, how about lunch, sometime soon? 521-9898, G.*

At 3:00 p.m., Lisa anticipated Tom's impending bark and lowered the volume on her phone. Then it came.

"Can you get in here so we can go over next week's schedule?" She heard the line close. Without hesitation, she stood, grabbed her steno and Mont Blanc pen Tom had brought her from his trip to Europe. She walked to Tom's office and stood in front of his desk. Tom was reading his paper with his back to Lisa when she walked in. Tom put down his paper, spun around in his chair to face Lisa.

"I'll be gone next week and the week after as well." He handed her a short stack of paper with details of what she needed to get done while he was away. That much she expected. "Any questions?" Tom asked.

"Good, that will be all." Tom stated after a momentary pause. He turned his back to Lisa, snapped his newspaper and carried on reading as if she wasn't in the room. Lisa left the office with instructions in hand.

At fifteen minutes after five, Lisa had put away the last of the day's work and slid the file cabinet drawer closed. She had slipped on her coat and was going to reach for her purse to leave when Tom stuck his head out of his glass office door.

"Have a good couple of weeks. I know I'll be enjoying my time away from this shit-hole. Oh, and don't forget Wednesday's presentation on the quarterly earnings to President West. I'm counting on you." He sneered and closed the door to his office without waiting for a reply from Lisa, or expecting one. Lisa snatched her purse and as she walked out she was thinking what a fantastic break this was this going to be without *Mr. Wonderful* in the office. She had already left a message about lunch with Gina.

Tom stayed until six p.m. and worked on the spin for Wednesday's presentation. He posted the presentation file to Lisa's calendar with specific instructions on where to find it and left his office.

As he rode his bike towards his exclusive condo overlooking the downtown and river, all he could focus on was his trip to the Eagle Cap Wilderness. He was getting away from his daily grind for the solitude of the wild. As he neared 44th avenue he knew he was only minutes from getting the hell out of town and would be off on his journey. As he turned the corner a large rough haired, yellow eyed dog crossed the road. Tom nearly careened into a black Jaguar sedan parked curbside. He glanced back to scream at the dog and it was gone. He yelled back anyhow.

"Damn dog!" He continued on his way dismissing the animal.

The following Wednesday, after presenting Tom's report to the company President, Lisa was complimented for her professionalism and ability to make Tom's second-rate revenue outlook presentation sound like it had hope. President West was the first to notice, followed by the remaining governing board. When she was done with the presentation and the remainder of the day's work, Lisa got into her car and her phone rang.

"Oh, hi Gina…Yeah, lunch tomorrow? Noon at Kells Pub would be great!" See ya' then." As Lisa headed out of the parking lot, she wondered what Gina had in mind. Attorneys don't invite you to lunch for the sake of eating. She wants information, Lisa concluded. But what could be said about Tom she didn't already have figured out. She wondered if she needed some inside information on Cooper & West. Regardless, it would have to wait until tomorrow.

At 11:55 a.m. the following day, Lisa arrived at Kells Pub to find Gina sitting with another finely dressed woman. This woman wore a very classy Armani two piece suit and Gina was dressed likewise in a fashionable Valentino. Lisa approached the table. Gina stood and introduced her law firm's president,

Amelia Newman. Amelia was an attractive dark haired woman in her early 50's. She was adorned with an elegant gold chain necklace with a large dark sapphire setting that matched her bracelet and her piercing eyes.

"Pleased to meet you, Amelia." Lisa replied and smiled as the three women sat.

"Well, Lisa, I bet you're wondering why I invited you here for lunch and brought along our President."

"Yes, I did wonder why, and felt it was important to come and find out what information you are looking for. Gina and Amelia looked at one another then back to Lisa. They all recognized it was more than only lunch.

9   Load Up

If we have no peace, it is because we have forgotten that we belong to each other.
Mother Teresa

The afternoon air at the Boise Airport was stifling on this July afternoon. Flight 1721 from Atlanta via Dallas had touched down with Katy and Sissy on board. As soon as the wheels were on the ground, Katy was on the phone getting a case update from Nelson. Katy started to talk to Nelson when the tall, sassy blonde stewardess that had been servicing the first class travelers snapped at Katy.

"You can't be calling on your phone until this plane is safely at its..." She was stopped short as Katy flashed her CIA identification badge and continued her call. The brazen blonde turned and walked towards the microphone to announce gate instructions without another word to Katy.

"Nelson." He was on the line within two rings.

"What do you have for me Nelson?" Katy asked. She anticipated new information which had been painfully slow in coming. The sluggish delivery of quality information was the very reason Katy had convinced Directory Kelly she should go on the wilderness trip. Katy felt the journey to find the very source of spiritual and cryptic information would give her the insight so her case could gain some new footing. Without on-the-ground knowledge of the crosses and rifled bullets, Katy felt there would be very little to truly rely on. She trusted her instincts and knew local knowledge could lead her in the right direction.

"I got a call from our Phoenix field office about half-hour ago and Officer Ben Manuelito had some insight that he thought may help. His family is from the Navajo reservation in the Four Corners area, you know, where Colorado, New Mexico, Utah and Arizona meet. Anyhow, he reported that he remembered seeing a swastika shaped cross with a man and spider many years ago. It was at the home of his grandfather. So Manuelito called and talked to his grandfather about this cross. In short, he reported that this type of cross was used in ceremonial gatherings where they would pray for rebirth and connection with the animal spirits of their world. The cross is made of bone to connect man to Mother Earth. The spider symbolizes spiritual understanding and the swastika shape represents balance." There was a long pause from Katy, before she replied.

"So how does this help us, Nelson? What does this have to do with the Secretary of State?"

"I'm working with Cultural Resources and our Phoenix office to get you answers Katy, this is all new ground for us." Nelson replied to Katy.

"Report to me as you find more and I'll keep you posted as I find further information as well." Katy closed her eyes and tossed her head back in pallid exasperation. Sissy looked at Katy and thought, this girl needs more than a vacation. She needs some real healing.

As Katy and Sissy found their way to the baggage claim area, Flight 2023, a De Havilland DH 114 Heron fourteen seat plane was on approach and landed. This flight had eleven souls on board which included Shelby and Curt. Curt constantly looked out of the plane, grinning like a dog riding with his head out the window of a car for the first time. He had once before flown in an airplane during a high school trip but had since been grounded at home in Ode. He was excited and brimmed with a level of enthusiasm he hadn't felt in years. Shelby on the other hand was less than pleased she had arrived. She felt she was somehow going to be able to weasel out of this trip, but wasn't able to. Shelby noisily flipped through the on-board flight magazine. Not reading it nor considering the Rosetta Stone advertisements for learning Spanish or other foreign language she would never use, nor the overpriced foot massager or flight pillow. She was infuriated by the fact that she was in reality going to the woods with no shower, no cell phone, no bed and no anything! She turned to Curt as he sat neck cranked nearly out the oval Plexiglas window and smacked him on the arm with the now rolled up magazine. She glowered and pointed with her French manicured finger towards Curt.

"You know Curt, this is your fault. If you wouldn't have come over to my parent's home and agreed to take this god forsaken trip to god knows where, I wouldn't be here! But no! You had to agree. You just couldn't say no! I hate you!" Curt was astounded by Shelby's attitude. He was silent for a second. Then he calmly replied.

"Now, we both know it was your idea that I come on this trip so you wouldn't be alone. You also convinced your dad and mom to let me tag along at their expense. Maybe you need to be more careful of what you wish for, because you might get it." Shelby scowled silently with contempt for what seemed like an eternity to Curt. Deep down, she knew he was right and found herself at a loss for words. She turned away from Curt and threw the rolled magazine in the aisle. They sat in unpleasant silence. The fasten seat belt light turned off with a single quiet ding. They deplaned without another word.

"Hungry?" Shelby finally asked Curt.

"Yep." The two sat and ate without talking to one another. Shelby realized she was headed to Oregon and couldn't back out. Curt smugly smiled inside. He was excited and looked forward to a grand adventure.

It was 2:09 p.m. when the old, faded, green four-door Ford truck pulled into the arriving passenger terminal with a 20-something woman at the wheel. The truck came to a rattling and squealing halt. Everyone waiting at the arrival curb turned and looked at this out-of-place truck that seemed as if it should be displayed at a farm auction rather than serving as curb-side limo service. What made it special was that it was unmistakable. It was the very truck that both Sissy and Shelby recognized from the wilderness travel booklet. Sissy, Katy, and Curt and Shelby started moving towards the stopped truck. The driver was dressed in a snappy red and white plaid shirt that had seen its better days in the sun. Her saddle worn blue jeans and leather boots that were reminiscent of the decrepit boots Festus wore in the old Gunsmoke re-runs. Her long auburn hair was tied back in a neatly combed French braid with a brightly colored hair band at the tail end. As they arrived at the truck, the woman driver walked to the curbside.

"Hi, I'm Pati and I'll be driving to the trail head and will be going with you to the Eagle Cap Wilderness. You must be Leslie." She recognized the willowy woman Jackson Red Heart had described.

"Yes, I am, but please, call me Sissy." Leslie replied.

"Sissy it is. Welcome." Pati replied.

"So, you must be Curt." Pati looked at the only man in the group, noticing his nice smile, blue eyes, and broad shoulders.

"And, Katherine Roberts?" Pati looked at the other two women, seeing who would respond.

"Katy." She replied as she subtly raised her hand.

"So that must make you Shelby." Pati and Shelby exchanged polite smiles. "Well, let me get your gear loaded." Pati easily heaved the oversized luggage Shelby packed into the bed of the truck. She then loaded the three remaining small bags.

"Lets load up, we've got a ways to go." Pati said with a beaming smile. Katy was seated in the front passenger seat with Sissy right behind her. Shelby sat in the middle and Curt behind the driver. The old Ford was well worn, but clean and comfortable, something Shelby would have never expected. The four door truck easily accommodated the four guests and Pati, who looked into the cracked side view mirror as she pulled away from the curb and into busy traffic. They exited the airport and headed westward on I-84 towards Oregon and their wilderness adventure.

10   Ten Rules

We do not understand when the buffalo are all slaughtered, the wild horses are tamed, the secret corners of the forest are heavy with scent of many men, the view of the ripe hills blotted by talking wires. Where is the thicket? Gone. Where is the eagle? Gone. This is the end of living and the beginning of survival.
Chief Seattle, Dwamish - Sugampsh

It was a brisk and misty morning. Jackson Red Heart had loaded and tied Bright Moon, the last of the mules who had packed in the kitchen and food supplies for the trip. The other mules, Two Whistles, Little Wolf, and Little Thunder, were all ready to go with the necessary supplies to keep everyone fed and happy for the next two weeks. The supplies were an addition to the trip Jackson had taken the day before. The previous trip supplied the kitchen provisions, stoves, and all the needed equipment to keep everyone content. Included on Bright Moon's load was a Sunday night dinner that would likely prove memorable.

The other four mules in the pack string included Black Bird, White Eagle, Two Rivers, and of course, Tank. He was named Tank after Agnes L. Vaaknin, a portly country woman, who had retired after 37 years of teaching grade school. She, five summers previous, while out on a wilderness trip with Jackson, was out on an evening walk and got stuck waist deep in a muddy meadow. Mr. David Vaaknin came hollering back into camp.

"My Aggie is stuck in the muck and she's sinking, she's sinking." Jackson, in an ever-calm disposition didn't say much, merely walked over to Tank, or Tall Tree as he was previously known, haltered him, grabbed a rope, and followed Mr. Vaaknin.

"Now, where's your misses Mr. Vaaknin? Ol' Tall Tree will get her out of whatever mess she got herself into." Jackson asked Mr. Vaaknin as he started up the trail with Jackson and Ol' Tall Tree trailing at a steady clip. When they arrived at the clearing, beyond the quaking aspen, there was Agnes. She was nearly 100 feet off the trail and waist deep in the mud created by a mountain spring.

"Mr. Jackson is here to save you Aggie." Mr. Vaaknin yelled out to Agnes. He was careful not to get too close to her. Jackson made a simple lasso, put it around Tall Tree's neck, tossed the dumb end of the rope to Agnes and called out.

"Now, put the rope around your back, up near your arm pits, tie a double half hitch up front and hold tight." Agnes did as she was asked. She put the rope around her back, tied the rope in a double half hitch as Jackson had explained and held on for dear life. Tall Tree pulled and Agnes was promptly drawn from the muck with a squeal like a happy hog at feeding time. Luckily, Agnes Vaaknin had a good jacket on or that rope may have left a healthy burn mark. The rest of the night, all she would say, repeatedly, to the guests was: "Tank goodness for da' good ol' mule. He saved my life. Tank goodness, tank goodness."

Agnes had carried on with such exuberance as if a great miracle had been performed, when no such an event had occurred. Jackson thought it would only be appropriate if Tall Tree be honored for 'saving the life' of that fine woman. Jackson honored the event by giving Tall Tree with the name of *Tank* following that humorous event.

At 8:11 a.m. everyone was gathered at trail head near Jackson Red Heart's old green Ford and horse trailer. Everyone had their gear. Some had plenty and some, more than plenty. At least that was Jackson's impression. With all guests present, Jackson started with his Ten Rules Talk which focused mainly on what not to do.

"Rule one." Jackson blurted out. "I'm in charge! If you think you have a 'good idea,'" making invisible quotes in the air with both his hands, "clear it with me first."

"Rule two," he continued, "respect your horse and your horse will do the same. And believe me, all the horses know rule two." There was a quiet laughter. Everyone looked around seeing who was really paying attention and guessing who wouldn't follow this rule.

"Rule three is don't take off alone. Not one of my guests has died and it is up to you to keep this streak alive. Always partner-up." Although Sissy and Katy and Curt and Shelby were partnered, Father Herrera found it easy to join anyone. Jackson continued without interruption. "Number four. We are here to enjoy and learn from the wilderness, so leave Mother Earth as you found her. Number five. If you manage to misplace yourself and start wondering which way back to the bread and bacon, be like water, go downhill. You're bound to run into a traveled path where someone can find you." There was an unnerving long pause as he looked at everyone.

"Rule six is important. Don't believe everything you see or feel here on the mountain. The wind, trees, sky and shadows hide secrets you may not understand. These are spiritual lands with many mysteries and deep unknowns. Trust what you know to be true – don't listen to the voice of the co-yo-te." There was complete silence, as Katy and Sissy looked questioningly at each other. Jackson noticed the blank stares and continued without further explanation or pause.

"Rule seven. Always carry water with you if you leave camp, even for a short while or a short walk. Rule eight. We are strangers now, but soon to be friends. Treat everyone with complete respect, honor their experiences and open your heart to learning from them and the mountains. Rule nine. If you stand near your horse's ass, she will either shit on your shoes or kick the crap out of you should you accidentally spook her. Either way, she wins. And one last rule, the cold night air, big skies and wild spirits makes for unusual dreams. Listen to your bones and your life force. Be aware of balance between the spiritual, natural and supernatural elements of the world." Everyone was speechless and quietly fearful of what they'd gotten themselves into.

"As I call your name, come to me and I'll introduce you to your horse." Everyone gleamed with excitement.

"Father Herrera." Jackson said loudly. He stepped forward. "Everyone, this is my long time good friend, Father Ricardo Fernando de Herrera. He goes by Father and will be bringing up the rear as he has done many trips before. Listen to his words." Jackson handed him the reins of Bear, a nine-year old gelding appaloosa that was cinnamon and white in color, broad chested and majestic as horses come.

"Father." Jackson continued. "Why don't you show our fine guests how to properly mount their horse." Father took the horse a few feet from where the group was standing in a semi-circle, grabbed the reins in his right hand, placed the same hand on the saddle horn. Then placed his left foot in the stirrup, and with a light bounce of his right leg threw his right foot over the back end of the horse and positioned his right foot in the stirrup.

"Simple as that." Jackson said. "Katherine Roberts." Katy raised her hand and walked towards Jackson. "Okay, Ms. Roberts." Jackson started but was courteously interrupted.

"Oh, just call me Katy, all my friends do." Katy said, smiling at Jackson while taking the reins of Big Sky, another tall and handsome appaloosa.

"Now, Katy, this is Big Sky." Jackson held Katy's hand open and outreached so everyone could see. Big Sky snorted and sniffed Katy's hand.

"Big Sky, take care of Katy, okay?" Jackson spoke sincerely at Big Sky, and Big Sky seemed to understand, Katy thought.

"Go ahead and line up to the right of Father and he'll show you how to tie him up and get you set to ride." Katy took hold of the reins, and walked alongside Big Sky, perceptive of the fact he was in charge of the ride and not the other way around.

"Garrett!" Jackson hollered. Shelby Garrett begrudgingly stepped forward.

"This is Red Blanket." Jackson said in a calm voice. "This mare knows the mountains and trails better than I ever will." Shelby cautiously held out her hand so Red Blanket could get a whiff of her. Red Blanket blew out a handful of clear, watery snot. Shelby was not amused. She withdrew her hand quickly and wiped it unenthusiastically on her new jeans.

"It's like you're sisters now." Jackson said as he grinned then pointed to Big Sky.

"Go line up to the right of Big Sky." Shelby apathetically grabbed Red Blanket's reins and walked over to her spot in line, cautiously, still wiping off her wet hand with that 'ooo-gross' look on her face.

"You must be Mr. Moore." Jackson said, as he was the only man standing where the others had gathered round.

"Curt" Curtis introduced himself by coyly extending his hand to introduce himself. He had done this, following Katy's lead.

"Well, this is Mound of Clouds. What he ain't got in big, he's got in brains, and you'll be following me. So, be sure to keep up and so you know, I don't talk a lot." Jackson handed Curt the reins and directed him to his line-up location.

"Ms. Jackson." Jackson called out. Sissy stepped forward, extending her hand and introduced herself as Sissy to Jackson.

"You're the singer from the South. I hope the cold nights are a welcomed relief from the heavy Georgia night air.

"I'm sure it will be, Mr. Jackson. I can't wait to breathe the high mountain air." Sissy said in her very southern drawl then smiled at Jackson.

"This is Rippling Water." He said, handing her the reins and directing her with a simple hand gesture and saying nothing else. Rippling Water walked towards Mound of Clouds with Sissy tagging along with reins in hand.

Jackson untied the reins of Big Wind, a wild-eyed mustang that was new to the trails. She was rideable, but only with a seasoned hand. Jackson then took the reins of Gray Feather, a beautiful ebony and spotted gray appaloosa that he had trained especially for the mountains. He took the two horses to the lineup. Tied Gray Feather at the lead and took Big Wind to the rear, where she would trail.

Jackson watched as everyone carefully prepared for the ride, making sure everyone had their gear properly secured. Ensured stirrups were set to the right riding length and the saddle cinch was secure. Everyone new to riding nervously mounted and found their bearings on their respective horse.

"Now relax and let them do what they do best! Don't pull up on the reins this will only get you thrown. Relax and enjoy the ride." Jackson, then mounted on Gray Feather, moved to the lead position. As expected, all the horses and riders moved in unison following behind Jackson's ebony and gray appaloosa, oblivious how their dreams and lives would change.

Behind the group of seven were the four kitchen mules, Two Whistles, Little Wolf, Little Thunder and Two Rivers. They were followed by the supply mules, Bright Moon, Black Bird, White Eagle and Tank, bringing up the rear. The mules were led by three hands who would manage the stock and kitchen. They had been handpicked by Jackson about a decade ago and they take better care of their guests and stock better than any around. The lead hand was Pati, as she managed the entire kitchen and was charged to ensure everyone was well fed and happy. Second is River, the best horse and mule man around. And third was Dilo, niece of Father Herrera, and she was the best trail and mountain gal these mountains had seen in many years. She knew the mountains well, as she has been living the summers here since she was tall enough to ride. She was the go-to gal for all the native foods, herbs and history of the mountains.

Gray Feather led the group of five mountain guests. They had traveled up from the parking area, past the trailhead wilderness signs and along the creek that rippled serenely alongside the trail. After they had traveled about a mile or so, Jackson stopped Gray Feather and tied him to a birch tree. He proceeded to check everyone's saddle as they stopped. Jackson tightened up a couple of saddle cinch straps but the rest seemed to be okay for now. As the group chatted, Katy was first to notice, or more accurately, feel, that something in shadows seemed to be watching them. She didn't 'see' anything, simply felt a presence among the shadows. She recalled what Jackson had said about being careful of what you believe you see, but this was altogether a strange life force sensation. She scanned the hillsides around her, saw nothing that stood out, but this was completely unfamiliar territory. It certainly was not the mock urban training grounds of Quantico nor the urban sprawl she was accustomed to.

"Father?" Katy asked. "Do you feel that *something* is watching us?"

"He is always watching us." Father Herrera gestured with his one hand and eyes looking to the sky.

"Not someone, but something." Katy quickly replied, with mild frustration, as she continued to scan the hills.

"Remember what Jackson said, don't believe everything you see or feel as the mountains hide secrets you don't yet understand." On that note, Katy decided to drop the talk, but continued to scan the slopes as they rode up the trail. Occasionally she sensed that someone or something was watching them. It was that stalker feeling that most people naturally sense when things aren't quite right. She was looking for an elusive lawnmower man, circling his prey. Jackson had said, 'don't listen to the voice of the co-yo-te,' Katy thought to herself. She kept alert as the morning cool dew transitioned to powdery trail dust and ribbons of hot sun shining between the tall trunks of trees. It was no wonder Jackson said to always carry water, the lingering trail dust alone would choke a camel, Katy thought.

11 Uncommon Good Will

We are taught to believe that the Great Spirit sees and hears everything, and that he never forgets: that hereafter he will give every man a spirit-home according to his deserts....This I believe, and all my people believe the same.
Heinmot Tooyalaket, Chief Joseph - Nez Perce

Office of Senator M.C. Phillips. Room 1303, a conference room with massive Brazilian cherry conference table, 13 leather executive chairs, embossed writing pads, silver Waterford pens and crystal water glasses, each filled with ice. The meeting started at 15:01 EST. Senator M.C. Phillips began the dialogue with her Chief of Staff Jack Burton, and two staff tribal liaisons.

"Gentlemen, this is our opportunity to make history. Our goal is simple. Get our tribal partners to allow the mining of both their salt and extensive zinc resources. This will be good for their tribes' failing economies and for the mining unions. We need to sell it and sell it like syrup to their tribal councils. Is this clear?" Senator M.C. Phillips' intention was for the councils to partner with NYSERDA (New York State Energy Research and Development Authority) via her office, then sell their salt and zinc ores to China, India and Pakistan for the manufacturing of cheap chemicals and auto parts, an ever-expanding market in China and India would support this endeavor. Pakistan's interest in specialized zinc alloys are for military application in their intercontinental ballistic program. Senator M.C. Phillips wouldn't offer too many details until she received the forthcoming agreements from Cooper & West.

    Senator M.C. Phillips continued. "Our first agreement will need to be with the Seneca tribe for their salt mines. We need to sell them purely on economics, even though our intentions are much broader. They need not know the scale of our objectives nor the goals of our international partners at this time. We'll acquire the rights to their mineral resources and gain access to their land at shall we say less than a premium. The partnership contrasts provided will offer us a very lucrative opportunity while giving the tribes a seat at this table of opportunity where we govern the rules of the game. Now work your magic so we can get this deal sealed. Secretary Vance, Senator Holden and Congressman Cussler don't like to hear about delays and for the love of God, no leaks to the media. This could really be shit on our face if the media gets wind of our intended goals with our international partners at this time. Remember gentlemen, contracts first then the rewards will come." She placed her index finger over her red pursed lips and emitted a viper-like shhhhh.

Both tribal liaisons from the Senator's office departed on separate chartered flights to both Seneca and Oneida tribes to begin to work their charisma with the tribal councils. The first presentation was given to the Oneida Tribal Council. The economic picture the liaison painted was astounding. What the Senator's staff promised were long term ore contracts, improved wages, greater control and more environmental safeguards for the zinc mining and smelting process. The same economic rewards were offered to the Seneca Tribal council, plus they added long-term post-mining contract use for storage of sensitive records and related resources in the geologically stable sites.

The tribal councils listened with eagerness to the significant potential for economic development they dearly needed. Yet they were equally cautious. Both councils questioned the undesirability of long term occupation of their lands and the all too clean and polished appearance of their proposals. One councilmember stated the need to be cautious and never give a devil a ride because the devils will always want to drive. This mistrust discouraged the

Senator's tribal liaisons and they called in Jack Burton to help smoother over the divided councils.

The Seneca and Oneida each held tribal gathering to have discussions, bring blessings to their respective tribes and their lands. For two days and two nights they conducted meetings, held prayers, and meals in honor of their forefathers, the spirits of their ancestors' land and for the future of their tribes. The gatherings ended with the tribal councils being both applauded for their vision and mistrusted for their impulsive desire for profits by their people. The people of the Oneida and Seneca tribes were divided. There were also the shamans who were not convinced of the uncommon good will and mistrusted the offers extended to their tribes. They felt the disquieting blanket of deception being drawn over the eyes of the councils. Their words of admonishment went unrecognized by some members of their tribal councils but were indeed heard clearly by the spirits of their ancestors.

12 Nal-Geen Bottle

Every gun that is made, every warship launched, every rocket fired signifies, in the final sense, a theft from those who hunger and are not fed, those who are cold and not clothed. This world in arms is not spending money alone. It is spending the sweat of its laborers, the genius of its scientists, the hopes of its children. This is not a way of life at all in any true sense. Under the cloud of threatening war, it is humanity hanging from a cross of iron.
Dwight D. Eisenhower

Tom Bade had made his solo trip from his downtown Portland luxury condo to the rural countryside of Wallowa County in rugged Northeast Oregon. He stayed at Chandler's Inn, a comfortable and relaxed Bed & Breakfast mostly suited for executive adventurers or a couple's hiatus. He crassly insisted on a 5:30 a.m. breakfast of fresh fruit, freshly squeezed OJ and dry wheat toast. Tom's early hour request did not sit well with the B & B's owners, but they begrudgingly met his request. The clock in his Buckingham Blue Range Rover radio beamed in bright red-orange 5:57 as he headed out towards the trailhead, a short 17 miles up a wash-boarded gravel road. Tom bitched the entire way up to the trailhead to no one in particular as he sped without much care to the world around him. When he reached the trailhead parking area, he took the first convenient place to park, designated for horse trailers only. He parked alongside a large green trailer and truck with horses and mules that waited to be unloaded. Tom grabbed his backpack he had meticulously prepared with everything for his trip into the wilderness. From his high quality Alpine tent to the hiking boots on his feet, everything was of the best quality and carefully picked out well in advance to meet any challenge the mountains might offer. This included his prized stainless steel and rosewood handled .22 cal Ruger, in case of snakes or other vermin. He haphazardly filled out the wilderness registration, and left off his destination, time in, expected time out, and headed up the trail. He hiked up the trail about an hour then stopped along an outcropping of rock over-looking the shaded stream below. He set his backpack down and reached for his Nalgene water bottle for a drink and found it missing.

"Damn-it!" He called out. Paused, looked in a couple other pockets knowing well it wasn't there but looked anyway and cursed out again increasingly louder each time.

"Damn-it, Damn-it, Damn-IT!" He looked around and found a large boulder on the slope beneath a large ponderosa pine and stashed his pack there so he wouldn't have to carry it down to find his Nalgene bottle. As he proceeded down trail he grew progressively infuriated at the fact that he had not found it. He was about half mile above the trailhead when he saw Jackson and the string of riders and pack mules headed up trail. As Jackson approached, Tom ignorantly stood upslope of the trail and started waving his hands in the air, yelling out to Jackson.

"Hey you, did you see a green Nalgene bottle on the trail?" Tom's movement spooked Gray Feather and Jackson brought him to an abrupt halt. This caused the whole string behind Jackson to come to a stop. Jackson wanted to keep this imbecile from getting every horse spooked. Jackson was annoyed by the insensitivity of this hiker.

"Mister, kindly step down slope of my horse and stop your yelling or he's bound to kick the shit out of you as we pass." Jackson called to Tom. "And no, there's been no sign of your *Nal-geen* bottle." The group of riders passed as Tom reluctantly stepped down slope of the horses. As they rode past, Tom purposely spooked Katy's horse by shaking the willow branch. They exchanged spiteful looks. She bit her tongue, changed her mind and she softly whispered under her breath. "Asshole."

Tom continued down trail, and had a few profane words as he stepped around and finally in a load of sloppy, warm and slippery horse dung. His few chosen words for the horses and riders were enough to turn the air blue as he proceeded on his search for the *Nal-geen* water bottle. It irritated the crap out of him how that cocky old cowboy said it, "Nal-geen."

Tom finally got to his Range Rover without finding the Nalgene bottle on the trail. He reached in his pocket for his keys and found it as empty as his character. He peered in the rear passenger window and there on the floor board, half-way beneath the seat was his green Nalgene water bottle. But Tom had no keys. He considered for a brief moment to break a window to get this water bottle but lack the testicular fortitude to damage his precious Range Rover. He proceeded back up trail, aggravated at himself for misplacing his bottle, forgetting his keys and now having to follow the fresh trail of horses and mules and suck up a little of the remaining trail dust dispersed by those *damn animals*. After a hike back up for his keys and back down for his water bottle, Tom ultimately arrived back to the place where he had originally stopped for a drink. He had some water and went to retrieve his stashed back pack. In the three or so hours he had been gone, a now long gone rodent had managed to gnaw its way through the exterior of the pack and into Tom's store of trail mix and pre-packaged energy bars. The mischievous rodent left more than one surprise for Tom as he would later find. The air beneath that large ponderosa pine was transformed to a brilliant bright blue and a few other shades to an unmentionable degree. After several minutes of gathering his well spread belongings and making readjustments to his pack, Tom was back on the trail questioning himself about this trip. As he proceeded up trail, Tom began to calm down as his attitude improved and he at long last started to enjoy the trip to 'his wilderness.'

13   Precious Blue Stone

You don't have a soul. You are a soul. You have a body.
C. S. Lewis – Irish novelist and literary critic

The string of riders had been on the trail for about two hours when Curt called ahead to Jackson.

"Hey Jackson, what's that?" Curt pointed to a mass of decayed flesh, dismembered bones and scattered fur. He thought they may be the remains of a long dead dog. They were lying alongside the trail, beneath the arching branches of a thorny pink wild rose.

"That is what remains of a mystical and deceiving Co-yo-te." Jackson replied, as he slowed to a near stop. Gray Feather did not want to slow down. He urgently and erratically moved up the trail with the other horses following nervously behind. They passed the foul carcass of the once living master of trickery. As they rode by, each rider curiously gazed down at the carrion, except for Sissy. Only she noticed the mass of creeping spiders, suspended in the thicket of the pink blossoms. There were hundreds of tiny dark spiders hanging on glistening strands and seemed to be waiting above the coyote as the group rode by. They made Sissy's skin crawl and she shivered lightly at the vision of so many writhing spiders.

"What did you mean when you said mystical and deceiving coyote when all we saw were his bones and fur?" Curt asked Jackson as they reached the crest of the trail. Jackson rode on for several seconds in silence, and then said, as if talking from another person's voice.

"My ancestors tell a fable. The coyote brings trickery and deceit into the lives of people. The coyote brings darkness where there should be light. Be aware of the shadows as that is where the coyote lies." For the first time on this trip, Curt was cautiously fearful. Not for his decision to come on this trip, but rather fearing what else he might have to face. This is only the beginning, he thought. He rode on and didn't ask another question of Jackson for the remainder of the day's ride.

It was near noon when they reached a stretch of trail that was narrow with dense vibrant willows on either side. The willows obscured the cold, glistening stream that meandered through the thicket of yellow stems, and crisp spring greenery. Mossy green and pumpkin orange lichen cliffs hung above the stream, nearly blocking out the afternoon sun.

This made for an ideal cool and canopied stop for lunch. Jackson walked to the tail end of the pack string of mules and retrieved the paper sack lunches. Pati helped distribute the full bags. Each rider found a shaded spot. They enjoyed their lunches and talked about what they each saw along the trail. Sissy grumbled about the dust and bugs. Shelby complained of the dust, bugs, smell of the horses, how the saddle made her knees hurt and of not being first in line, and the sun that was burning her near perfect complexion. Other than the little nuisances expected from city people, everyone else was enjoying the horseback trip. They each gave their horses the sweet carrots that had been packed in their lunch sacks. As they finished lunch, Jackson let them know they were about nine miles from their camp.

Along the trail to the camp, they had to ford three streams and one river that made Father Herrera believe in God even deeper than before. Plus they trailed along a few stretches where a fall would mean a most certain death. By the time they arrived at their camp, they were all tired, thirsty and saddle sore from the day's ride. As they entered the camp, Mound of Clouds, Curt's steed, did a sudden spin nearly sending him off his saddle, but he did manage to stay on. Curt was startled from his one-man rodeo until everyone gave a cheerful applause and complimented him on his horsemanship. Everyone except for Shelby, who claimed it was pure luck and maintained it was the pucker factor that kept him clamped to his saddle.

Jackson had each rider tie their horse in succession to dispersed horse hitches as they arrived to camp. He assigned the riders their private tent that was already set up in a large, informal semi circle. The kitchen was placed at one end and the communal fire-pit set near the center. The fire pit had large granite river rock forming a circle of about six feet in diameter and several wood rounds for sitting. There was also a primitive log bench, strung low to the ground making it an ideal place to warm as the frosty night air began to fill the camp.

Everyone went to their assigned tents to settle in for the stay. Everyone arranged their belongings to suit their needs. The tents were spacious dome style tents with substantial rain fly, interior pockets for books, flashlights and the sort. Every tent was set so the door was facing the morning sun so when they arose each morning they could greet the morning light. Stitched to the inside above each doorway, was a hand woven grass cross in the shape of a swastika with a white shell and turquoise bead sewn to its center. When Katy saw this she immediately thought of the third cross found at Senator George Cussler's home, but that cross was bone and had a man and a spider. Katy lit out of the tent, and went straight to Jackson and demanded in the very same voice she commands her staff of CIA Officers.

"Exactly what is the meaning and purpose of the swastika and beads in my tent Jackson?" Katy snapped. He worked at dismounting the saddles with River and brushing the sweaty horses and mules. Jackson didn't stop his routine, and didn't even look back at Katy, but felt her defiant stare. Jackson spoke in a soft patient tone, as a master would speak to his disciple.

"Every day, you awake in a concrete and steel box you call home. You don't greet the morning sun and kneel and touch Mother Earth. You don't feel the spirit of the ground, its minerals or its seas. You rush out and drive your iron beast on hardened roads from one empty box to another." There was a long pause. Katy was silent and patient, as she knew there was more.

"Here," pointing with a nod and brim of his well worn hat to the ground below him, Jackson continued, "here, you begin the day with wisdom. As you wake to greet the morning light coming through the door of your lodge, the cross is there to bring you balance from the four winds. This will help you find the direction and steadiness you must have. The precious blue stone, turquoise, comes from Mother Earth. The white shell comes from the waters that bring life to everything. Greet each day with respect for the earth and waters that give you and everything you are, a soul." Jackson silently continued his work on another horse. Katy stood quietly watching as he methodically worked on each stock animal. She grasped to find the greater understanding in the words Jackson spoke. She stood in silence for several minutes longer, contemplating whether to dig deeper and interrogate Jackson for more information.

"Thank you." Katy finally said. She stayed for a second longer wondering if she should ask more, and then wandered back to her tent in thought. She crawled inside, turned, sat, and stared up at the woven cross with greater interest and circumspection. She remained there for several minutes, investigating the detail and considered the symbolism of each piece and what they meant holistically. As she studied the cross, she considered that the other cross was made of bone and this one of woven grass. She wondered what the significance of the woven grass was. And this cross had turquoise and shell and the other, a symbol of a man and spider. Why she pondered. The Christian cross, was inscribed with a coyote and the Gila Monster which further confused their meaning. Katy instinctively knew there was a relation between them, but what was it? She was deep in reflective thought when she heard a piercing scream.

"Spider!" No coincidence, Katy immediately surmised. But was she simply jumping to conclusions to fit her thoughts or was there more. She quickly got out of her tent and went to check on the source of the blood chilling scream. It was Sissy. Sure enough, there was an itty-bitty, brown spider near the door of her tent. Katy reached down and in one swift brushing move, scooped the attacking arachnid from Sissy's tent. Sissy was incredibly grateful for Katy's speedy actions, gave her hand a squeeze, and nervously squirmed at the thought of the huge spider, in her mind.

"I do a lot of things Katy," Sissy spoke, "but I don't do spiders. They make my skin crawl something dreadful."

"Don't hesitate to call if spiders are bothering you Sissy, they don't bother me a bit." Katy replied. Sissy didn't say anything, just looked at her in child-like disbelief that there was a girl on this big blue earth who didn't fear spiders.

When it was time for dinner, everyone walked slowly, sorely and hurting in places they didn't know existed. As Curt walked up to the chow line, Jackson waited to greet each of his green guests.

"I never knew a saddle could make a man's ass so raw." Curt said.

"Just wait." Jackson replied without a facial expression and flat panned.

Curt was again fearful of what was certainly to come.

For dinner, Pati had prepared everyone a cowboy cut, flame cooked, garlic infused flat iron steak, Dutch oven Idaho baked potatoes and the freshest mushroom and native asparagus anyone had ever tasted, as both came from the mountains. Sitting on one of the stumps near the granite fire ring was a large bottle of cabernet, brought for this fine, first night dinner. Nearly everyone had a glass or two by the end of the meal. A steak dinner of this sort would typically taste good, but something about the cool evening mountain air made this meal exquisite. Pati and Dilo cleared the dinner dishes and a round of applause ensued for the fine meal they had prepared. Shelby and Curt added several logs to the fire as they were enjoying the fire a little *too* well. All through dinner both were having quiet and private conversations and making flirtatious gestures and body language as amorous young people often do. They both decided to take a late evening walk and proceeded beyond the circle of campers. Their voices could be heard well as they walked past the burning glow of the campfire light and up the trail. They had been gone only for a short while when they ran back down the trail, very much out of breath.

"Jackson, there is something up there. It was following us on the slope as we went up trail. When we would stop to see if we could spot it, it would also stop, at least the sounds stopped." Curt blurted.

"And it seemed to be all around us." Shelby said, regaining her breath. "It was not only in one spot. As we were walking, I thought it was to my right and Curt thought it was behind us and to his left. We stopped a couple of times and it would stop too. Then we both saw the shrubs and grass on the slope move, first up the trail and quickly on our right and then down slope on the left. It scared the crap out of us and we decided to get the hell out of there and fast." Shelby was nearly in tears.

"Tell me Jackson, what in the hell is out here? Tell me, I need to know!" Shelby demanded. Curt put his arm around Shelby and Jackson stood at the same instant. Everyone else was visibly bewildered by the event and listened in silence. Jackson stepped towards Shelby.

"Everyone, now. Let's keep our heads about this." Jackson said, and then continued. "These mountains are the home to many animals. There are bear, deer, mountain lions, coyotes, and many other animals that become active at dusk and dawn. Wolves are known to have traveled here from the east. I have been seeing and hearing these wild animals for many decades and they do not wish you harm. It is good that you two were aware of your surroundings and came back when you felt danger. There are many spirits in these mountains that you need to be aware of as well. Trust in yourself. Only you can give your fear permission to control you."

"Damn it Jackson, I know there was something there, we simply couldn't see it. It was watching and moving very, very fast along the tree line. It seemed to be anticipating our moves. Now tell me, what the heck is out there mister?" Curt demanded as he was not in a mood to hear a bunch of psycho-woods-babble, Curt more than wanted answers, he needed answers.

"Well, you felt it was anticipating your moves and moving fast. There are myths from ancient times of spirits that move with the winds through the peaks and valleys of these winding waters. These spirits are the souls in the eternal struggle between spider and coyote. The spider creates understanding in the mind of man and the coyote counters with deception. This conflict occurs in a void that exists between the spirit of the living and the phantoms of the departed. It happens on the winds and faint shadows we usually cannot see. It is like trying to explain what pushes the winds. We know the winds move, we simply can't see what is pushing and pulling them across the land. This is where the spider and coyote exist, in the plane between what is real and unknown; the coyote pushing you into deceit while the spider is pulling you out. You may have been witnessing the fast moving spider countering the elusive and shadow dwelling coyote. It is fortunate you did not become entwined in their battle. Now that you are here, you are safe from their draw, for now."

As everyone listened to Jackson's explanation, they realized in their individual ways that there was more to this wilderness experience than camping and riding horses in remote northwest mountains. There was an incomprehensible aura about this place. For some, an unimaginable journey would begin that night.

14 The Offer

I think somehow we learn who we really are and then live with that decision.
Eleanor Roosevelt – Civil rights advocate and author

Lisa waited for Gina or Amelia to start the conversation. She wanted to establish what information they were truly going after. Gina began.

"Lisa, last week when I was at Cooper & West and several times before, I noticed what a professional you truly are. Tom informed me you would be presenting his report to the president this week, and in his words, 'hoped you wouldn't screw it up'. But what I had in mind on Friday and what I have in mind today, well, has changed a bit. I would like to discuss an offer our firm has should it interest you."

'Well, that is why I'm here?' Lisa thought to herself, but instead asked Gina.

"So, what is your offer, Gina? What are you really after? You know if it has to do with Cooper & West, there is confidential client information I can't disclose."

"No, no. It's nothing like that. What Amelia is in search of is a new Executive Assistant and knowing what good work you do we thought you would be an excellent fit for her needs." Lisa felt somewhat shocked they knew anything about her skills and abilities.

"You mean to tell me Tom actually said something nice about my work?"

"Both Gina and I have known Tom and Mr. West for a number of years. We know what a difficult personality Tom is to work for. I spoke to Mr. West and discussed this opportunity and Mr. West is the person who recommended you to us." Amelia added. "Tom, on the other hand, would only say a good word if it was about himself, that smug blue eyed son of a bitch. Gina wanted to speak with you first, but another pressing issue developed yesterday, before Gina called you. So are you interested in considering this position? And of course we'll match your current compensation plus thirty percent."

"So what issue developed that made this offer pressing?" Lisa asked without pause. Again, Gina and Amelia looked at one another then back to Lisa, realizing her keen intuition.

"First of all, I need someone of your caliber. Someone that is able to think on the go and take care of details." Amelia explained. "My firm requires attention to detail and someone to go the extra mile when necessary, and quite frankly you have already demonstrated that today. Secondly, we perform some contract work for various government organizations that require confidential inquiry." She concluded.

"You're telling me you need some inside information on Cooper & West for the IRS? Sorry, I already told you that I can't disclose information about our clients." Lisa replied. Gina then again entered the conversation.

"Lisa, hon, it's bigger than the IRS and we're not looking for you to disclose any client's personal information." Just then the waiter walked up to the table and asked if they are ready to order. Ever polite, Gina shifted the conversation to ordering lunch, leaving Lisa wondering what in heaven sake do these women truly want and what price they are willing to pay.

The waiter took their order and left. The conversation continued with Lisa taking the lead.

"So, you need access to information you feel I have permission to retrieve. Yet, if I go to work for you, I won't be able to get any information from Cooper & West. To be honest with you, I'm really not at all comfortable in giving away information I'm not entitled to give." Then Amelia pulled her chair closer to the table and spoke in a whispering tone.

"Lisa, this is the way it works. You come work for us, but before you actually report, you give Cooper & West two weeks' notice. In your last two weeks there we only need to know one thing about Cooper & West. Deal?"

"Well, it really depends on what you are looking for." Lisa began. "Cooper & West have been good to me. I can't say much about Tom, other than deep down he is not entirely evil just arrogant as hell. But, I do have my loyalty to Cooper & West and my integrity needs to remain intact." Gina and Amelia again gave a momentary glance at one another.

"Yes, we understand your need to maintain your integrity and we wouldn't ask you to compromise that. What we are looking for is nothing that typical confidentiality policies include. We're not looking for anyone's personal information so you'll be fine." Gina added. Lisa listened intently to both Amelia's and Gina's proposal, but didn't hear specifically what she did need to give them. They were silent, waiting for Lisa's approval. The waiter came back to the table with their drinks, set them down and walked away. He recognized he had interrupted their hushed conversation.

"Well, now, Amelia. Be specific with me. Exactly what *one thing* do I need to provide you that Cooper & West obviously has?" Lisa asked.

"Now dear, if I told you what we needed before you are fully on board, it wouldn't be very clever of me, now would it? Amelia replied. There was a brief pause then she continued. "What I am offering you is a lucrative promotion, solid benefits, and a way out of working for that prick." Her voice softened. "Let's make this a win-win situation. You can give my offer full consideration and call Gina by six this evening. You let her know of your decision and if it is mutually beneficial, we'll meet, discuss details and move forward. How does that sound, dear?" Lisa was somewhat taken aback by the sudden change in Amelia's tone and the ambiguity of the offer.

"Yes, Tom is a prick, isn't he?" Lisa remarked. They all laughed. Lunch arrived and they finished their meeting. After lunch Lisa returned to work at Cooper & West, captivated as to what Amelia was truly after.

15 Yellow Canines

You must speak straight so that your words may go as sunlight into our hearts. Speak Americans. I will not lie to you; do not lie to me.
Cochise - Chiracahua Apache

At 3:30 that same afternoon Tom came upon the *damn horses.* They made his hike up the mountain one of minefield avoidance, which deep down angered Tom to no end. As he walked by, both Shelby and Father Herrera waved at Tom, not recognizing him from earlier in the morning as he now had his oversized pack, sun glasses, and a hat on. He damn well recognized them and hiked on without an acknowledgement of any kind. Father Herrera noticed the hard and ruthless nature of Tom's soul and silently prayed for him. Tom continued on the trail not needing to be mindful of the horseshit and welcomed the lack of lingering dust.

As Tom hiked around the next rocky rise, there was a spectacular panoramic view of an alpine lake ahead. He watched the sun and shadows played their magnificence on the granite stone turning it a subtle shade of rose. He stepped into a fresh laid pile of what smelled like dog crap.

"Wonderful. Fuckin' wonderful!" He shouted in disgust. He tried to scrape the stinking feces off his boot onto the green fescue. Out of the corner of his eye he saw movement. He stopped the shoe scraping and turned to look and saw nothing, but was a little startled. He continued to scrape and then again saw what had spooked him in Portland. It was the same *dog* that he had nearly run into when riding back to his condo. But, how? He questioned. How could it be the same damn dog? He watched the dog's yellow eyes as it stood with its broad body filling the width of the rocky trail. It then vanished. Tom, now filled with trepidation, started to question if he really saw the dog. Was it really there? He looked all around and saw the empty trail. He looked down to continue to clean his boot, but it was completely clean.

"I'm freakin' losing my mind." Tom said out loud. How could the dog crap be there one instant and gone the next? He looked around as if someone was playing a cruel trick on him. There was no one. He continued his hike up trail, constantly scanning ahead of him then looking behind for the shadow dog. Tom rationalized it was the long trail and stress from work.

Tom stopped on the trail and inspected the lake below. He dropped his pack and reached in to the top exterior pocked to retrieve his wilderness map. He pulled it out, acquired his bearings as to his location and determined he would set camp on the southeastern edge of Moccasin Lake. This is what he had been dreaming of while stuck behind his desk and having Lisa, push paper that suited her dim intelligence. We all have our place, he thought, and hers is behind her desk and mine is here.

As he traveled down slope to his waiting lake he planned his evening. Tom decided he would set up camp, fish until nearly dusk, build a fire, eat fresh trout and get a really good night's rest. As he rounded the last switchback on the trail, there was the dog. Crouched. Snout wrinkled. He showed his oversized yellow canines. His determined low-pitched growl, raised hackles and sinister yellow eyes made Tom stop cold in his tracks. He could smell the canine's dirty, wild musk. Instinctively, Tom stepped back, trying to lengthen the space between him and this devil looking beast. The dog kept his ground. Tom retreated, five, then ten, then thirty feet back. Tom turned to run and another beast suddenly appeared upslope on the trail.

"Oh – crap!" He gasped. He was trapped. Tom fished for his .22 caliber Ruger from the side pocket of his pack. He could feel his trembling hand around the cold barrel, but couldn't dig it out of its tight quarters. Both dogs sensed his fear and started moving in. His hands fumbled and face sweated profusely. The growling beasts moved in, one paw in front of the other. Slow. Patient. Hunting him. Tom finally had his Ruger out, pointed at the beast upslope, and pulled the trigger. Nothing happened. The pistol's safety was still on. "Fuck!" He yelled out. Off went the safety and he pulled the trigger again, this time the pistol rang a loud echoing clap. The dog didn't flinch, and worse, it was still moving forward, slow, hunting. Tom fired the Ruger again to no effect. The two dogs were now within three yards, he turned and fired a third round, this time at the dog down trail and the dog, again, vanished in a puff of fine gray vapor. He turned to again fire at the dog upslope merely to see the same fine cloud of gray vapor dissipating. True terror filled him. Bewildered, he fell to his knees. Tom tasted blood's iron bitterness.

16   Melancholy Rain

Dreams surely are difficult, confusing, and not everything in them is brought to pass for mankind. For fleeting dreams have two gates: one is fashioned of horn and one of ivory. Those which pass through the one of sawn ivory are deceptive, bringing tidings which come to nought, but those which issue from the one of polished horn bring true results when a mortal sees them.
Homer – The Odyssey

A slow, drenching, melancholy rain fell outside the darkened room Sissy slept in. All felt serene and she could hear the steady, soft spattering of the rain on the tin roof that created a quiet hum. There was only a fragment of silver light coming into the room from a far away opening set high on the wall. From the light, she could hear the voice of her momma reading to her as she did when she was young.

"Br'er Mocking-Bird sings in de live-oak shade A secon' hand chant or a serenade; He'll take off a pa'tridge, a robin, or a jay, But he'll uver make a name no other way, But he ain't by isself in dat, in dat- But he ain't by isself in dat." It was a verse from the old poetic southern author Ruth McEnery,

Stuart's Mocking Bird. She heard the verse once, then again and then a third time. Each time she heard the voice of her momma with her mind drifting further and further back to a time when she was near seven years old. She could feel the soft voice that profoundly warmed her heart. Sissy knew her voice was coming from another place in time. She instinctively wanted to move towards her voice coming from the sliver of light. She struggled to get loose of the imaginary tethers that held her. She realized she couldn't get any closer to her momma's voice.

There in the recesses of her past was emptiness and fury wrapping into a tight ball of metal that had hardened her. What was causing this heaviness and uncanny grip on her, she wondered. Why couldn't she move closer and why wouldn't her momma come into the room with her? Sissy struggled in her dream.

"Momma, I'm in the room. Come in the room with me. Come through the window and down the lit stairway." Sissy yelled out. But there was no reply, only the gray monotone spattering of the rain came cascading through the sliver in the wall.

"Sing me the Mocking Bird momma, sing me the Mocking Bird." She cried out. There was no Mocking Bird, just the rattle of the rain. She sat and listened, trying to unbind herself. Then, very quietly, like an echo through the light started the chanting of souls. Far away and deeply touching were the tribal chants, calling and vibrating loose the restraints that kept her from the sliver in the wall. The chanting persisted and she became increasingly weightless. The light coming through the opening in the wall grew from a rainy sky gray to an iridescent blue.

The hypnotic shine of blue light mesmerized Sissy. It gave her a sense of calm and connection as it faded slowly from blue to a soft opalescent white light. The chanting grew louder and now seemed to be coming not through the sliver in the wall, but from the walls themselves. The vibrations surrounded her and simultaneously freed her from the grips of emptiness she had felt since her momma passed on. She could feel her presence in the room. Sissy never saw her momma, merely felt her in the rhythm of the nocturnal chanting. Not her voice, but her soul.

Sissy was reaching with out-stretched arms to the light when she saw a single silvery white thread of light beaming down towards her. The strand of warm light was nearly at her fingertips when she reached out and took hold of the light. She saw the white spider and it drew her towards the sliver in the wall. She wanted to let go, as she was fearful of the white spider taking her slowly towards the brightening white light. As she neared the opening in the wall, she could hear the rain serenely falling on the tin roof. She suddenly awoke with both arms stretched out towards the tent's vented opening. The near full moon was peeking down through clouded skies into the clearing of the semi circular ring of tents. Then she realized she had been dreaming and it wasn't her momma singing her the Mocking Bird. Sissy slowly brought her trembling hands down over her now ashen eyes, blocking the night's cold moon and alone, deeply wept.

17   Moonlight Bounce

The stars are putting on their glittering belts.
They throw around their shoulders cloaks that
flash like a great shadow's last
embellishment.
Wallace Stevens – American modernist poet

Morning had come quickly for Father Herrera. He had been first to go to his tent the night before. He had said his evening prayers, read for upwards of an hour and settled in for a pleasant night's sleep. A night of good restful sleep and dreams did not come for Father Herrera. For others it was a night of fearful visions.

Shelby listened from the refuge of her tent to every little chirp the night insects made. She heard the wandering winds as they rustled trees in the distance. Shelby felt as if she could hear the moonlight bounce off the tent's rain fly after her frightful experience she had on her evening walk. She didn't sleep much and when she did it was neither restful nor peaceful. She had a lucid dream of floating above the ground. As she ascended, she could see the horses, trees, and a creek flowing below her, as well as the semi-circle of tents. She floated through a light layer of moist clouds. She reached out and felt the cool, wet sky on her face as she climbed. Above here were brilliant star-filled skies like millions of clever ideas sparking all at once. Below her were the misty white clouds of a child's dream. She stopped ascending and remained weightless, overwhelmed with warmth and bliss. Subtle green lights appeared around her that were reminiscent of northern lights. As she floated in the vast timelessness, there began a rhythmic heart-like beating that emanated from every direction, including from inside of her.

    Shelby felt the beating in her body and head at the back of her eyes. The green skylights began to pulse with the rhythmic beat of the sky that surrounded her. Each pulse was slow, steady, and peaceful as if being in a womb. Thump, Thump-Thump, Thump, Thump-Thump, Thump. A tremendous feeling of wholesomeness and peace engulfed her every thought and emotion. In those timeless moments of peace came an instantaneous luminous flash of red lights directly above and below her. It was instantly, morbidly violent, shocking and soulfully disturbing. She felt herself falling as if suffocated by a thunderous blow and abruptly awoke in her tent. Shelby was wide-eyed and gasping for air. The air felt hot, sticky and nauseating as vomit. Shelby had no idea what had caused the peaceful dream to start, stop or why it came to an end so unexpectedly. She tried to catch her breath and as she sat up, she noticed a single spider scurrying away. She looked at herself as she was completely soaked in frothy-like body sweat. The kind of sweat you find under a saddle when a horse is ridden long and hard. Little did she know that she was not the only person experiencing this nightmarish psychological violation. Shelby grabbed her towel from her bag, first wiped dry her face then the rest of her drenched body. She was trying to figure out what the hell was causing such horrific dreams. She could barely breathe considering the morning was cool and the morning cast of light was starting to peek through the treetops.

Shelby calmed herself and changed into a clean tee shirt and pants. Then came a sound from the camp of someone aggressively trying to catch *their* breath. She sprang out of her tent and into the early light. Shelby listened intently and moved towards Curt's tent. Being aware not to disturb others, she called to Curt in a hushed voice.

"Curt? Curt are you okay? She was just outside Curt's tent. She listened to him as he gasped for air as she had scarcely a few minutes ago. She reached down, unzipped his tent and found Curt laying face up in his bedroll, shirtless and in a pair of briefs, nearly suffocated. She reached in and pulled him by his hand to an upright position.

"Breathe, Curt. Breathe God damn it, breathe!" Shelby yelled at Curt. His eyes rolled opened slowly, as if coming out of a deep coma. There was a look of near death in his eyes. Curt was pale, lifeless and unfocused, but breathing, barely. Shelby heard people in the background starting to unzip their tents one at a time. She felt a hand on her right shoulder.

"What's going on out here? Is everything alright?" It was Katy.

"It's Curt, he can't catch his breath. Curt was still shallowly gasping, as if having an asthma attack.

"I'm... O... K... Ca... n't... Breathe..." Curt spoke between gasps of air. Curt took a couple of hard breaths then continued. "Bad... dream... I ... guess."

"It's okay Curt, it's okay. Don't talk, just breathe." Shelby said in a deeply caring and compassionate tone. She held his hand tightly. Curt slowly caught his breath and gradually regained his composure. He was embarrassed about making a scene and everyone seeing him in his skivvies. He too, was covered in frothy sweat. He dried off and dressed then came out of the tent where he found everyone milling about. Most of the campers were still dressed in their sleep clothes. When Curt stepped out of his tent they all stepped towards him with a look of great concern.

"Curt, you gave us quite a scare. Are you all right? What happened?" Katy asked.

"Well, I was dead asleep having this peaceful dream of flying or like hovering in the sky as in an out of body experience, I suppose. I was watching these cool green lights in the sky, like the aurora, and hearing a beating drum and all of a sudden a flash…" Shelby cut him off and finished his thought.

"Of bright red lights came that were violent, shocking and deeply disturbing."

"How did you know, Shelby?" Curt asked uneasily. "And then I felt like I was being suffocated by hot air and I woke up in a haze and I could barely breathe."

"I know Curt. I had the very same dream. I woke up all full of that thick sweat and that is why I was up. I heard you when you woke up and couldn't breathe." Everyone was terrified at their experience. Then from the back of the group came Father Herrera's voice.

"Curt, Shelby, you're not alone, I also had the same dream early on, after I fell asleep. But when I awoke there was a spider, moving fast away from me, as if frightened."

"These dreams, they are there to bring people together that have the same challenges in their lives." Jackson said. "You, Curt and Shelby, you are both young. What do you fear? And Father, my good friend, what do your fears have in common with Curt and Shelby's? You should talk about your fears and you may find a common thread to unwind your worries."

"Jackson, can you tell me, how can these three people be having the same dream?" Sissy asked. "What is it about this place that can make somethin' like this be happenin'?"

"The spirits that live here in the mountains are very alive. Some bring confusion, trickery, deception and some even bring the dreams that we share. Other spirits bring direction, balance and understanding. It is a riddle we must discover and relate for ourselves. The spirits show us the way to turn the disorder to balance, deception to direction and trickery to clear, mindful thoughts. Miss Sissy, Katy, Curt, Shelby, Father and I as well, must find and distinguish between our shadows of fear and the light of our life force.

"You know," Sissy added, "Jackson is right. I had a dream about my momma who is gone from this heavenly earth. She came to me in my dream. But what also came to me in my dream was a white spider." Shelby gasped, but didn't say anything and let Sissy continue.

"This spider reached down to me with her shimmery white silk and tried to pick me up from my deep loneliness I've had since her passin'. The things I see similar in our dreams that they started calmly and ended sadly. One constant is the white spider in the end. Now, what is that little spider trying to tell us? I simply think that little critter knows something we need to know."

Everyone stood quietly in the cold early light. They thought about the dreams they shared, the words of understanding and consideration that Jackson and Sissy spoke of. They could not come to grips with the bewildering dreams they had in common. They did fine solace in the close friendships that had strangely formed. Jackson had told them of wild spirits that made for unusual dreams, but this was far beyond their understanding.

18   Dream of a White Spider

The American Indian is of the soil, whether it be the region of forests, plains, pueblos, or mesas. He fits into the landscape, for the hand that fashioned the continent also fashioned the man for his surroundings. He once grew as naturally as the wild sunflowers. He belongs just as the buffalo belonged.
Chief Luther Standing Bear – Oglala Souix

It was 6:53 p.m. when Tom decided he had hiked through enough of the dust, dogs and trail for the day. He eventually found a suitable spot to make camp for the night and proceeded to unpack his gear. As he began to set up his tent he noticed generously gnawed holes. The air became brilliantly blue from his foul words. Through the still of the evening air his voice could be heard echoing off the giant granite cliffs. His cacophony of ill spoken expressions would have made the ears of most of the mules and horses prick up with attention, albeit the nearest ones were one valley away. Tom mended and patched the holes in his new tent for the better part of an hour. He hoped for little or no rain, as there remained a hefty hole in the rain fly that was ill repaired in anger and frustration. The night was cold as a Siberian nun, and then it rained. Tom's eager plan of fishing, a fire, and eating trout had passed.

Despite the cold and rain, the interior of the tent stayed dry. The sleeping bag and pad had survived the rodent's wrath unscathed. As Tom slept, he began to dream he was riding his new Bianchi bike on the smooth streets of Portland towards home. The road gradually distorted from a slick pavement to rough gravel. He was being chased down the gravel road by the dog that had chased him before. The road became rutted and wash-boarded to the point that he lost control and crashed. He got brutally scraped on the angular gravel. His right hand got ripped from wrist to elbow exposing flesh and bone. As he reached in pain for his bloodied arm the dog that chased him began to viciously maul his face and neck. Tom felt the dog repeatedly biting, pulling, and brutally tearing him apart. He screamed and thrashed with every torturous bite. Tom screamed for help, but his cries rang into the night, unanswered.

Tom awakened to the moon filling the tent with frosted light. He reached for his bloody arm only to find no blood, no pain. He felt his face and neck, as he fully expected to find his hands covered in blood, and feel the pain of the dog's bites, but again, there was no blood. The pain that was real subsided as he realized it was a dream. He then saw his new sleeping bag was shredded at multiple areas which weren't there before he went to sleep. Or so he believed. He sat in a genuine James Brown cold sweat as his head and heart pounded. His soul soaked cold as the mountain night. He tried to comprehend the insanity of his dream and questioned if he was becoming delusional. How did his bag get torn and why is he not hurt. He questioned.

Tom heard approaching steps. He held his breath and listened to the hot-heavy panting of a dog outside of his tent. He was numb in his frozen sweat. Tom again listened to the dog's heavy breath outside of his tent to his right. He slowly reached for his pack at the foot of his sleeping bag. Trying to move as little and be as quiet as possible. He reached in and grabbed a hold of his .22 Ruger. Held it in his out stretched hands, trembled in fear of what he would be facing. He heard the dog, but now it seemed to have moved further to his left. Tom aimed the pistol in the direction he thought the panting dog was at. He pulled the trigger. Tom heard the dog behind him, then almost immediately to his left. He panicked. Shot off another round then quickly another. There was silence. No yelp. No scampered dog. No nocturnal sounds of any kind only complete and utter dark silence. Tom experienced the terrified, stinging, helplessness of trapped prey. He would not sleep.

Before sunrise, still shocked, he quietly unzipped the D-shaped door of his tent. Reluctant, he peered out to see what, if anything was shot or lying dead around his campsite. With his Ruger still in-hand, he cautiously emerged and scanned in every direction.

"Nothing. Freakin' nothing." Tom said aloud. He looked for tracks, blood, anything that would lead him to what he had experienced. But there were no signs of any kind. How could that possibly be he again questioned himself. Was his dog attack was a dream? But his bag was now ripped. Seeing nothing, he looked back into his tent to verify the condition of his gashed bag – but it was not ripped, not shredded at all. He searched for the bullet holes he shot through the tent wall. There were none. He checked his surroundings for the dogs and realized how frightened he really was. For the first time ever, he felt out of his element and out of control. He packed his gear haphazardly and was headed down-trail five minutes after he had come out of his tent.

Tom had hiked, more accurately, jogged down the trail for about an hour. He kept a vigilant look out for the dogs that haunted him. He came upon the campsite of the horse riders and mule pack string he had passed yesterday. Not being right-minded, he slowed as he passed. The group enjoyed breakfast and drank some comforting hot coffee. Jackson was the first to notice the hiker from yesterday and invited him over.

"Mornin', you're up and runnin' early. How-a-bout a cup of Pati's mountain brew to warm you up?" Tom nodded his head in agreement.

"Yeah, yeah, a coffee would be good." Everyone around the morning campfire nodded and greeted Tom as he sat on an empty log, closest to the fire.

"What's your name? Jackson asked. Tom had that far-away-look in his eyes and Jackson asked him, "You doin' okay? You're looking a little rattled on the edges." Tom again nodded his head.

"Tom. Yeah, yeah, coffee would be good." Tom said.

"Did you hear anything odd last night? Like dogs?" Tom asked. Everyone shook their heads to say no, except for Sissy.

"I didn't hear any dogs but I had the strangest dream of a white spider." Sissy said. Katy wanted to hear more and pressed her.

"Spider? What was your dream about?" Sissy proceeded to tell everyone of the odd dream of the white spider and how it reached down through an opening in the wall. What she left out was the part of her momma. It was too personal to share. She then finished her abridged version of her dream.

"It was one of those dreams that are so real that it gets to you, you know?"

"Yes, I do know." Tom answered. All eyes were on Tom.

"I had a dream that I was attacked by a dog. It was so real that it woke me. I heard it outside my tent and shot at it." Tom added.

"Now, where exactly did you camp last night?" Jackson asked.

"Just past Snow Creek." Tom replied.

"Well, if you were that close, we would have heard your gun go off when you shot. These mountains don't hide gunshots, especially during a quiet night. Did anyone hear gunshots?" Jackson asked. Some silently gestured no, while others spoke up and said they didn't hear anything. Tom then reached in to his pack that was at his feet, pulled out the Ruger and released the magazine. As he inspected it, he realized that the magazine was still full. No rounds had been expended. The chamber was clean and he couldn't recall seeing or picking up the brass from the rounds he thought he had shot.

"I know I had a disturbing dream. Maybe shooting the pistol was also a dream." Tom said in disbelief and sheer confusion. Everyone looked at

Tom and gave one another wide-eyed glances. Then Father spoke up.

"Dreams can often seem so real because they come from deep conflict within our minds. It is difficult with some dreams to discern fact from fabrications. Dreams can bring out the greatest joys or the deepest and most dormant fears. But after all, they are only dreams."

Father's explanation put no one at ease. To Sissy and Tom their dreams were terrifyingly real. Their dreams were built on foundations of fear which were slowly being exposed by the erosive winding waters of this spiritual place.

19   Shadow People

....all things share the same breath....the beast, the tree, the man....the air shares its spirit with all the life it supports.
Chief Seattle, Dwamish - Sugampsh

The following evening in the wilderness lead to an exhilarating delight. The night patiently unveiled a jeweled sky with the shimmer and depth of fiery black opal. It was a night of true wonderment for Katy as it was unlike any stargazing she had experienced. The night air grew uncomfortably cold so Katy decided to retreat to her tent. She read a while and listened to the peaceful sounds of the night.

Katy changed into her sleeping clothes. She thought of how she was going to explain this experience and its relationship to her ongoing case. She opened her sleeping bag, and adjusted her clip-on reading light. She sat for a few moments longer and analyzed the day's events. She wrote what she needed to report back to Nelson, but as she wrote her descriptive one line notes, she was surprised how sleepy she became. It was unusually quick she thought, dismissed it and tried to write on.

She nodded off with her reading light still on and started dreaming rather abruptly. Her mind raced as she began seeing changing colors, as looking through a kaleidoscope. The colors spun rapidly, coalesced then grew into distinct shades hypnotically slower and slower. She heard mild chanting and awoke. Alert, she listened for the chanting. Katy realized she had fallen soundly asleep. She sat up and listened for several minutes and heard only the sounds coming from the night breezes and crickets playing their nocturnal tunes. *Cheekity-cheekity. Cheekity-cheekity.*

With mild uncertainty, Katy fluffed her pillow and turned off her reading light. Feeling the cold, she secured her sleeping bag to the zipper's close and fidgeted, as she tryed to get comfortable. She remained awake for several minutes and listened to the c*heekity-cheekity, Cheekity-cheekity* and slowly dozed off again, unexpected - unknowing.

The dream started again. Rapid changing colors of boreal lights filled her dream, progressively slowing, slower and still slower. Emerald green tints fading to canary yellow. Then growing to crimson and neon blue then became more complex as colored fractals. The chanting started, coming from a long distance away. It seemed as if the life forces of these spiritual lands were chanting from long ago. The chant came from all directions and created a sense of calm and security like the warm woolen blanket around a baby. The dreamy fractal colors continued and the chanting persisted for several minutes. Colored skies faded in and out in intensity as chants grew closer as oncoming waves of water hitting a sandy beach with more waves behind each successive one. As the colors faded from hue to hue, shadows of animals began to appear as muted silvery-gray shadows. First a large dark bird appeared. A very large shadow of the bird was far off then nearer, screeched loud and sent shivers through Katy. Then the shadow of the cougar arrived. Slow, crouched, and hunting in the light between the gradual changing colors. As she stirred, she saw ghostly gray phantoms and continued to hear the far off chanting. The coyote appeared close by and moved with purpose, unfaltering, gliding. It was followed by a scurrying white silk spider, a spiny lizard and the eerie shadow of a man. Then bright colors melted into thunderous chanting and the shadows of many people circling appeared. They were the ones chanting. Their mouths moved. Loud, screaming at first, then the voices of the shadows grew softer. The hollow faces of children appeared. They were solemn and staring directly at and through her. Empty. Katy felt their sorrow.

The chanting again grew louder. There were more shadow people dancing. She heard beating of leather drums and screams of children. She then saw the faces of children flashing in and out between the colors of embers and fire. Katy was paralyzed. Suddenly, the drumming and screams diminished and the fires were replaced by similarly colored sunset skies and the animal shadows returned. First the shadow of the spider following the coyote, the spiny lizard and the human shape in a sun wise direction, circling as the wind of change push and pull. Chaos filled the skies as it expanded to a vivid white. From the depth of the pure white came the eyes of a woman. A woman's eyes she had seen before in dreams. Deep in the eyes of the woman she could see the silhouette of trees. Warriors moved through the foliage with arrows in hand, war painted faces, chanting and primal. As they moved she could see their feathered spirits and their ghostly white eyes. Fiercely bright, then fading, shadows of feathers moving among the trees and fading in and out as their chants grew louder then soft. Then the kaleidoscope of colors faded in slowly and soothingly calm. They grew from brilliant red and emerald green into soft blue and ruby pink hues.

    Katy suddenly awoke. She lay there motionless as she listened to the echoed sounds of her dreams, her fast beating heart, and the *cheekity-cheekity, cheekity-cheekity* of the night. She felt as she had dreamt for no more than ten minutes then recognized it was near dawn. Once she realized she was in the safety of her tent, she swiftly sat up and fumbled through her bag, looking for a pen and paper. First finding the pen, she reached for the novel she had been reading, opened the back cover and started writing feverishly: colors, chanting, spider, coyote, warriors, and eyes – woman's eyes. She stopped, thought for a brief moment, and recalled her dream of the gray ghostly shapes of people, the haunting shapes of animals and, of course, the vacant faces of the children. Her emotions overcame her at the thought of the sorrowful children and she wept.

    Katy sat alone and for the first time in many years was very afraid of her own dreams. Katy gathered her emotions and climbed out of the tent, but this morning, she greeted the dawn and purposefully touched the damp morning earth with both her hands as she exited. She thought about what Jackson had said when they first arrived about greeting the morning sun and Mother Earth. Mother Earth - she thought to herself. Were those the eyes of Mother Earth? There was to be greater purpose in every day.

As soon as she got out, she went directly to Sissy's tent and knelt down near her doorway.

"Sissy? I need to talk to you." Katy whispered. Sissy had been awake for some time, listening to the cold calm of the morning. Sissy immediately noted the urgency in Katy voice. The tent's door zipper moved quickly drawing open the tent.

"Come in. Come in." Sissy told Katy. Sissy moved to let Katy in. Katy zipped the door to the tent shut and held Sissy close to her in a much needed embrace. Katy then began to tell Sissy of the dream she had and the deep sorrow in her eyes and the tears on her cheeks told the rest of the story.

"These dreams! There is more to them and more about this place than I understand because I've never had dreams like these." Katy finished. Sissy nodded in acknowledgement.

"What I told you about my dream was only a part of the dream. The rest of it was too painful to share with anyone. In my dream, I heard the voice of my momma but she wouldn't come to me and I couldn't reach or see her. But she *was* there. There is more to my dream and more to come. I feel it." Sissy added.

"I know. I feel it too." Katy replied. "I know there is more to my dream that I haven't figured out or don't quite get. I'll have to wait and see what happens tonight. Sissy, I'm truly afraid of what I may find out."

20   Sacred Thunderbird

They made us many promises, more than I can remember, but they kept one; they promised to take our land, and they did.
Red Cloud, Mahpiua Luta - Oglala Lakota

As soon as breakfast was finished, Jackson and Pati got all the day's provisions that included lunch for everyone. Jackson packed a satellite phone for emergencies, in case anyone had a *good idea,* his .30-06 caliber rifle and plenty of water for everyone. Provisions were all loaded on one of his favorite day-trip mules, Bright Moon. Tom asked Pati if he could stay at their campsite for a while, gather his thoughts and then move on down trail. Pati agreed and informed Jackson. Pati was leery about Tom but made sure he had a good breakfast. Tom ate alone. He sat quietly by the embers of the morning fire. Tom continued looking around for his yellow toothed dogs.

Everyone was mounted on his or her respective horse and on Jackson's commanding double skip whistle they knew it was time to move up the trail. This day trip was going to take everyone up the draw they were camped in, over Lincoln Ridge, down Gunnerson's creek, and into the Mirror Lake basin. Everyone was told to expect less dust because of the granitic trail, more sun and a long day in the saddle. Curt now realized what Jackson had meant when he said, "Just wait." This will surely mean some sore knees and bums before the day would be over.

Sun at this altitude has a way of tanning your skin to a bright hew of ruby and leaves you feeling like fire is coming out of you. Many the folks coming from the Eastern states have skin that is not acclimated to the lack of atmosphere at this high altitude so they have a tendency to burn and often blister. This happens on those areas you typically forget about like your ears and neck. A couple of years back, Ol' Man Wilson thought he was rougher and tougher than the midsummer sun. After spending half a day out on the trail he was redder than fall pepper, and mad as hell from the blistering on his forehead and top of both oversized ears. There is nothing like a little aloe gel to cool those hot spots and burned areas though, and Pati had packed a bottle, in case it was needed.

As they rode through the valley, the vegetation became increasingly sparse as they ascended to the trail's crest. Once they reached the ridge, the riders stopped for a much-anticipated break from the saddle. They took a short walk and enjoyed the panoramic view of the Eagle Cap Wilderness. This was a delightful sight to behold, even for those who venture into the high country often. Brilliant blue-green lakes surrounded by bare gray-granite peaks, sparse patches of fir trees and life inspiring vistas in every direction. It's a place that envelops you into the wild landscape. The most remarkable thing everyone commented on though was the cool, crisp and stirring air. It was like taking a clean breath of air for the first time in your life. They all stood absorbing the vast and wild aura. Jackson pointed out Sacagawea Peak, highest point in the wilderness at an elevation of 9,838 feet, named after the Native American woman who led Lewis and Clark in discovering the Northwest for the U.S. government. Jackson also described the wilderness as sacred grounds of the Nez Perce who have occupied these lands since the 1400's, but most likely long before that. The lands were a hunting and gathering place where life and death were carried out. A land filled with the Great Spirit. Animals and man were interwoven into the fabric of this spiritual land for centuries. As they admired the rich history and landscape a loud thunderous sound came from the cloudless north. First they saw nothing then in the distance was a large dark bird flying high in the thermals of the mid-day sky. They all watched.

"Jackson, is that an eagle or a vulture?" Sissy asked in her harmonious drawl.

"Well let's watch it. We'll see if it comes closer." They all watched and gave their opinion as to what it was.

"It's a golden eagle, you can tell because its wings are level as it is flying." Shelby stated with new found authority.

As Father Herrera watched the bird fly above them, it seemed to be similar to the bird that rode the rising thermals above the burial mounds of his ancestors. He wondered if this bird was this the guiding spirit he sought.

"That looks so large. Are golden eagles really as black as that bird? Jackson, is there something else that it could be?" Katy asked. There was a hollow look in Jackson's eyes as he recognized what it was. He watched as the bird flew nearer. This was the benevolent and sacred Thunderbird. Rarely seen, it had been nearly fifty years since he last saw this bird when he was a young boy. Jackson questioned that after so many decades if this could this be the sacred and revered Thunderbird he dreamed of seeing again. As they watched, it came to rest on a jagged outcrop across the glacial valley. The riders could see the red fire in its eyes. The horses became unsettled and started snorting and acting as if a fierce power was among them.

"Jackson, what is that? Whatever it is it is way too large to be an eagle. It looks bigger than a man. It must be about seven feet tall." Katy stated. Jackson started backing up from his point on the outer circle of the riders.

"Grab your horses, mount up, and let's go! I'll explain when we get out of sight." Jackson commanded.

"Out of sight of that, that bird?" Curt spoke nervously.

"Get on your horse, and let's go." Jackson again ordered. They all fearfully mounted their horses as Jackson led them at a galloping pace down the slope to a rocky area that put a ridge between them and the Thunderbird. Jackson rode quickly, constantly looking back, ensuring everyone was coming along without straggling too far behind him. It appeared it was the horses that were most fearful of the Thunderbird. The horses and Bright Moon easily kept up with Gray Feather. Once they reached a rocky ravine shadowed by old growth fir trees, Jackson slowed Gray Feather for about one hundred feet then came to a stop, turned and raised his hand, getting everyone to stop their rush for cover. Without pause and from his mount he started talking as soon as Father Herrera, who had been at the tail end of the run, stopped.

"That, my good friends, was the sacred and powerful Thunderbird. His wingspan is nearly twenty-five feet and stands taller than a big man when perched. Some believe that the Thunderbird brings harm with his thunderous spirit and others believe he brings the wisdom, and sacred power to protect and guide people. I was only a young boy of seven years when I first saw this giant spirit. It is believed that he brings both the life giving water and crop damaging hail to our lands. He is revered and powerful and it is my feeling we need stay away from him. It is said that he can carry livestock and people away and I don't want to find that out today."

"Why did we run when he was still so far away?" Katy asked.

"Katy," Jackson spoke in a slow, knowing voice, "I do not know if we were in danger. I do not know if we were too close and I did not want to wait to ask. It is better…" Then there was a tremendous clap of thunder, which seemed to have come from the direction of where the Thunderbird was perched. Only a few seconds passed when his large shadow was cast over the riders as the Thunderbird flew high above the treetops. The horses were now thoroughly terrified. Mound of Clouds bucked and Curt spilled painfully to the ground. Sissy and Katy's horses ran off back up the trial in the direction they had come. Father's and Shelby's horses followed Gray Feather as he raced off the trail and through the trees in the direction opposite of the bird's flight. It was nearly a half hour before they all gathered together down trail. Everyone was clearly frightened.

"What we have experienced is a living spirit recognized by both the supernatural folkloric beliefs of an ancient myth and the heart pounding truth of what we've seen. We mustn't let our fears of our experience cloud our judgment." Father Herrera said.

"We must remain vigilant of our surroundings, be calm, and we'll be just fine." Jackson added.

"Just fine? Just fine?" Shelby spoke out. "We were nearly attacked by a monster black bird and you think we're *just fine*? Hell no, I'm not just fine. Between my dream and the Thunderbird, I want to get the hell out of this place." Katy realized that Shelby was frightened beyond belief and wanted to help her regain her composure. Katy dismounted her horse, and handed the reins to Sissy. She walked over to Shelby and reached her hand up to her.

"Let's take a walk." Shelby was either too afraid or too nervous to move but finally, reached out and held Katy's hand, dismounted, and walked off with Katy's arm around her shoulders. Shelby cried as she and Katy walked away from the rest of the riders. Everyone, including Jackson, kept watch on the sky to see if the Thunderbird would return.

About twenty minutes passed. Katy and Shelby returned from their talk. Shelby was still rattled.

"Jackson, can we head back down to camp? I think I need some rest. This trip to Mirror Lake was too much for me. I think I need to lie down." Shelby pleaded.

"Is everyone okay with going back to camp? Jackson asked the rest of the riders. There was an immediate and unanimous agreement of head nods.

"Yes." Both Father Herrera and Curt agreed simultaneously.

"Mount up and we'll head back right now, Shelby. Let's go!" Jackson concluded.

They all arrived back at camp a little before five p.m., were all quite tired from the long ride, and overwhelmed by the Thunderbird experience. The horses were also out of sorts as Jackson and his crew worked to get them all unsaddled, brushed out, watered, and calmed. Once everything settled and folks had the opportunity to clean up a bit and have a little down time Pati offered up a big plate of fruits, crackers, cheese, smoked salmon and opened a couple of bottles of a nice pinot noir which everyone quickly polished off. That evening there was a lot of discussion about their experiences, dreams, and emotions. Shelby spoke the least and realized that she wasn't alone in her fears of the Thunderbird.

"I really believed that I was going to die today. Sissy stated. "The way that big ol' bird flew slightly above the trees, and my horse just started runnin' and runnin wild. If that bird didn't kill me I knew that frightened horse would. My ol' heart was beating faster than those hooves were hitting the ground. So I decided I would die praying. I started praying and I guess that horse felt me praying and he finally stopped runnin'."

"The power of prayer is an amazing force Sissy. It has the power to calm even a horse." Father Herrera retorted and everyone laughed out loud.

At half past ten that evening, everyone had retreated to the quiet and comfort of their tents for a much-needed night's sleep. All except for Katy and Shelby, who continued to talk about their deepest fears beneath the silver stars, sitting next to the warmth of the glowing embers. Katy told Shelby about a time when she was not quite ten years old and she was visiting her aunt and uncle in Boston. She was sent to sleep in a large bedroom on the far end of their home. Her parents were there, but they were going to sleep on the second floor and she on the third floor of this palatial home. She shared the story with Shelby. "It was winter and my mom had sent me to bed while the grown-ups stayed up looking at old family photos, having a conversation about the Vietnam War, and how an uncle from Maryland had not been heard from in weeks. He was presumed to be alive because it had happened several times before, considering the secret missions he was routinely on. I had been in bed, although not asleep because I was too afraid to close my eyes. I remember lying under the warm and heavy wool blankets. I watched as the moonlight and barren branches from the giant maple tree made strange moving shadows on the walls. I was so afraid because I felt so alone in that enormous bedroom. I could hear all the little noises and it seemed like someone was watching me. After about an hour of tossing and hiding under the blankets with my flashlight and pillows, there was a creaking at the door. I so dearly wanted it to be my mom or dad coming into the bedroom. But all I saw was the face of a man peer half way through the closed door. It was like he was coming through the wood. I screamed as loud as I could. A few seconds later their maid opened the same door and right behind her was my mom and dad. I told them about the man's face in the door. I was so afraid of what or who it was. I begged my mom to stay with me, instead, she sent me to the room she and my dad were staying in. I finally fell asleep, but not until mom was in the bed with me.

The next morning after breakfast, my dad and uncle sat side by side at the kitchen table again looking at an old photo album of long ago relatives and friends. They were such curious pictures. I stood silently, and looked over my dad's shoulder at the photo album.

Then I saw this picture and yelled. That's the face that came through my door last night Daddy! Their faces became wide-eyed. They looked at one another then back at me.

Are you sure that was the face? Are you absolutely sure? My dad asked.

Yes Daddy! That was really the man! I remember seeing his little eyes, his round glasses and long sideburns, Daddy. I was so afraid and my dad knew it.

Please don't be afraid Katy. That is Uncle Michael, he couldn't have been in your room last night, he's on the other side of the world in Vietnam. He couldn't be here too, dad told me. That same evening as we were going to sit down for supper, my uncle received a call from my Grand-Dad, letting him know the Chaplain and another army officer from Fort Detrick had come to his house to let him know that Uncle Michael had been killed in action. That night there was a lot of crying in my aunt and uncle's home. There were a lot of questions asked of what I had seen the night before. Everyone believed me about what I had seen and asked if Uncle Michael had said anything and how he looked. But I didn't hear any voice. I remember seeing his little eyes behind those round glasses come through the door. There was pure emptiness in his eyes. I had never been so afraid of what I had seen and the feeling of the unknown that surrounded my thoughts. I had never felt that way again until today, when the Thunderbird flew over the trees, raking over us and there I was, again looking up at the unknown.

    Shelby reached out to touch Katy's hands and hold them as she trembled at the memory and today's mysterious Thunderbird experience. They both sat in silence for a few moments. Without saying a word, they both got up, left the campfire. Shelby went to her tent, pulled her bed-roll out and took it over to Katy's tent. They both eventually fell asleep, knowing they were better off having someone in the next bed-roll, at least for the night.

21   The Sins of Others

Brother, you say there is but one-way to worship and serve the Great Spirit. If there is but one religion, why do you white people differ so much about it? Why not all agreed, as you can all read the Book?
Red Jacket, Sogoyewapha - Seneca

The morning sky was a soft blue of glacial ice and the air was crisp. Katy was well rested, out of her tent and had gone up the trail, in sight of the camp below. From this higher vantage point she could see the burning embers from the prior evening's fire and Pati's tent glowing from her ready light. Katy was on the satellite phone talking to Nelson who had been at work early. He was preparing for her call even though she made no prior mention of time. It was one of those 'givens.' When Nelson answered his office phone, Officer Katy Robertson went right to work.

"Well, Nelson, here's what I have so far…" Katy went on to explain how some of the symbolism may tie in with the Senators, Congressman and Secretary of State.

"Look in to some of the hot issue items they are currently working on. Find out if any of the senator's staff are working with extremists or religious zealots. Check what policies they are working on. Look for coyotes and spiders. See what doesn't fit. See what may be out of balance."

Nelson thought Katy had lost her mind. "Spiders? Coyotes? What do you mean by out of balance?" Nelson asked.

"Sorry, I've experienced some rather unbelievable events in the couple of days I've been here. No time to explain now, but see if our esteemed New York Senators and honorable Secretary Margaret Vance have been up to anything out of the ordinary. Try taking a look at their issues from the viewpoint of policy of theirs being one sided. Check if their dealings with any of the tribal issues seem off-colored and not what they appear. Talk to Officer Ira Knight in Portland and field agent Manuelito of Phoenix and see how they can help. Something is not right with our representatives." Katy finished.

"We do know that Senators Holden, Phillips and Congressman Cussler recently traveled to the Seneca Nation to have discussions over mining and several lands issues. Also, some of the members of the Oneida tribe were also present. There was no mention of the Secretary Vance or her staff at this meeting, but I'll do some more digging." Nelson followed up.

"Nelson, why don't you give a call to Dr. Michael Ku. He was convinced his program on psychological profiling would work for us. Why don't you give him the information we are working with maybe he can offer some insight we have not yet considered. Also, have Ira from our Portland office give him the Native American spiritual background information as well."

"Great, I'll be calling you for an update this evening. I'm sure I'll have more by then. Good luck." Before Nelson could reciprocate, the connection went dead and Katy was headed down to camp to talk to Jackson about the bone crosses, etched spiders, Gila monsters and man.

The aroma of richly prepared coffee filled the camp air.

"It looks like the hiker set up camp with us for the duration. Do you know if he's okay?" Katy asked Pati as she poured a cup of coffee.

"Well Katy, since you asked, he seems a bit too weird for this gal."

"What do you mean, 'weird'?" Katy asked.

"It's like he is running from something, on drugs, or simply not right. That look in his eyes when he came into camp gave me goose skin. I've been working these mountains for many years, had some real different folks join us, or folks we met on the trail. But this one is a little spooky, even for my liking."

"He mentioned he shot at some dog and yet no one heard anything? Do you think that was remotely possible?" Katy asked.

"Up here, as Father and Jackson have said, not all things are as they appear. For example last fall we were with a group of seven tribal leaders from the Seneca Nation from New York, nice folks and all, but they claimed to be long ago children of the spirits from these mountains. They talked to the elders of the Nez Perce and a couple from the Jicarilla Apache were here as well. It was quite unusual that such distant elders meet. While they were here, there were some rituals that lasted nearly until dawn. Around three in the morning I was awakened by their chanting. Jackson, Father and the tribal leaders were in some kind of trance, talking in different native tongues I had never heard and…" then Jackson appeared behind Katy. Katy did not know Jackson was standing behind her and had overheard what Pati was saying. Pati went back to work.

"…And what? Pati what did you see?" Katy asked. Jackson then started where Pati left off.

"And Pati saw us speaking to our forefathers." Katy turned to face Jackson standing inches from her, staring through her.

"What is your purpose here Katy?" Jackson asked. "You have come not for yourself but to find the sins of others haven't you?"

Katy was speechless. "If you want to find the truth, asking Pati, the Father or me, you will not get what you are seeking. You will find only our perception of what we see as true for ourselves. Whatever you seek, you will find in your open mind and not in a clenched fist."

"I'm going to lay it all out real clear as to why I'm here. I need to find out why three U.S. Senators, a Congressman and U.S. Secretary Vance were sent a warning. They were each sent a .50 caliber round and ancient bone crosses. Help me understand Jackson, this is all I want." Katy demanded. Jackson was incensed, still looking through her.

"Katy, if that is what you seek, you can find it. You live everyday in the den of the coyote, yet you come thousands of miles to find him here? Your coyote is not here. Here, however, you can find what you seek, but you are looking with your eyes closed, hands clasped and your heart being deceived." Katy thought of what Jackson's words really said about her and what the symbols meant to her case.

"Yes, I do need to open my eyes to a new way of looking at your world, Jackson. I need the time to comprehend the relationships between the meanings of the animal spirits and my world." Katy then walked off, leaving her steaming mug of coffee to go cold in the morning air. Jackson turned as she walked away, fully knowing the meaning of what she sought, but it was for Katy to find.

Katy felt she was getting close, well, closer to understanding than where she had been. But there were too many unknown relationships she still did not see for herself. She sat on the granite stones looking across the camp to where weirdo Tom's tent was set. It was now past dawn and Sissy was headed to the coffee pot for a morning cup.

"Goodmornin'." Sissy whispered as she passed Katy.

"Mornin'." Katy responded without thought. Katy was thinking about weirdo Tom's look when he entered the camp. His eyes were dead. He had seen, heard or experienced something that scared the hell out of him, because before he was the asshole on the trail and something or someone changed that. Since then, he hadn't come out of his tent, as far as she knew. She walked over to Tom's tent and from about ten feet away she spoke.

"Tom? Good morning. Coffee is on and I wondered if I could bring you a cup?" All was silent in his tent. No rustling of sleeping bags, no breathing, no acknowledgement at all. She waited for a few seconds more.

"Tom? Good Morning. Coffee is on and I wondered if I could bring you a cup?" Still no reply came. Not a sound came from Tom's tent. She knelt and slowly unzipped the D-shaped door of the tent and peered in.

22   Crimson

Today, more than ever before, life must be characterized by a sense of universal responsibility, not only nation to nation and human to human, but also human to other forms of life.
Dalai Lama – High lama of Tibetan Buddhism

Office of Senator M.C. Phillips. Room 1303, a conference room with massive Brazilian cherry conference table, 13 leather executive chairs, embossed writing pads, silver Waterford pens and crystal water glasses, each filled with ice. The Meeting started at 10:01 EST. The only agenda item: Senator M.C. Phillips Memo that read as follows:

```
To: U.S. Secretary Of State
Margaret A. Vance, NY Senator
Claire Holden, US Congressman
George C. Cussler, Seneca Tribal
Council and Oneida Tribal Council
and NYSERDA Director.

From: Senator M.C. Phillips
```

Involved Parties: U.S. Secretary Of State Vance, Senator M.C. Phillips, Senator Holden, Congressman Cussler, Seneca and Oneida Tribes, Governor of NY & NYSERDA Director.

RE: Transfer of tribal mineral and surface rights.
All involved parties have acknowledged and signed legal transfer document of specified tribal hard mineral, zinc and specified surface rights to NYSERDA (New York State Energy Research and Development Authority) for immediate project implementation.

Chief of Staff Jack Burton stood in for Senator M.C. Phillips and began the morning meeting. He recognized and congratulated the involved parties in signing off the comprehensive energy initiative and program start date. He went on to state that there would be a formal announcement and appropriate press release in conjunction with on-site ceremonies at multiple locations in the coming weeks. Everyone was given a round of applause and symbolic pat-on-the-back for all their exceptional work on this mineral initiative. Secretary Vance would be announcing to the governments of Pakistan, China and India that mineral rights and new sources of zinc had been secured for exclusive global energy partners. In closing, the Jack Burton announced his departure from the Senator's Staff for an Energy Directorship position with the U.S. Secretary of State office coordinating international energy agreements and policy. Again ceremonious applause and symbolic 'you-earned-it' congratulations were offered by all present. This mineral and land agreement proceeded unnoticed beneath the public's radar. It was billed as a simple mineral agreement that would be good for the tribal economies and tribal union miners of New York and especially being mutually beneficial to all parties involved. The parties involved knew big money, big government and even bigger plans were intertwined within the legal sprawl of the 737 pages of agreements that were delivered via Cooper & West.

That same evening, Secretary Margaret A. Vance, Senator M.C. Phillips and the now former Chief of Staff Burton were all at the corner of 6th St. and Pennsylvania Ave. at The Capital Grill, one of D.C.'s famous steakhouses of the political establishment. Wine and appetizers had been served when by mere coincidence Mark Kelley, the CIA's Director and his wife Donna Kelley, were seated two tables from Senator M.C. Phillips' party of three. They went unrecognized. Mark and Donna were at this upscale establishment celebrating twenty-six years of marriage where he would present to her a ruby and diamond necklace after dinner. The ruby and diamond combination had always been one of Donna's favorites and such a gift was long overdue, Mark had concluded when he made the purchase. As dessert and a third bottle of wine was being served at the Senator's table, the Senator raised her glass and made a toast to, "sealing the deal," then carried on for several minutes of narcissistic oral diarrhea, as Director Kelley would later call her ramblings.

"If it were not for your great salesmanship and magnanimous word-smithing," she gleamed at Jack, "the Oneida and Seneca Nations would have never trusted this vital economic program." They all tapped the rims of their newly filled crystal wine glasses. They toasted, drank and set their glasses down.

After finishing his dinner and presenting Donna with his little shiny red gift of her own, they left the restaurant arm in arm. The valet brought his black Lincoln Towncar to the curbside for them.

"Before we leave Donna, I have a quick call to make to Officer Nelson." Director Kelly said. He dialed Nelson.

"Nelson, Director Kelley here. Look into the deals between the New York Senators and the Seneca and Oneida Tribes. There is a deal that really stinks. See how Secretary Vance is tied in. Got it?"

"Yes Chief. Anything else?" Nelson asked.

"Yes. Be sure Officer Roberts gets the details tomorrow and let her know I'll be expecting an update because the dogs on the hill will be barking expecting answers." The call to Officer Nelson lasted less than half a minute, then Mark and Donna were on their way.

Nelson had been at home when he received Chief Kelley's call. He dressed in a fresh white button down shirt, blue silk tie and dark navy trousers, black shoes and was headed to The Company. He made several phone calls to verify and gather more specifics on the Phillips-Vance 'deal'. At this late hour, information was slow in coming and was incomplete. A call to Katy with limited information, as this hour, would not be prudent, Nelson concluded. He wrapped up his calls and exited the glass door to the officer parking area. It was 2:17 a.m.

23   Bitter As Blood

My eyes are an ocean in which my dreams are reflected.
Anna M. Uhlich

Sissy awoke from a very peaceful dream of silver light shining through silk shadows. She was wrapped in momma's soft iridescent blue jacquard shawl and as she heard her singing, she hummed along. Sissy swayed slowly as the Spanish moss of the live oaks in a southern summer breeze. *Mmm, mmm, mmm,* her momma sang.:

"Br'er Mocking-Bird sings in de live-oak shade A secon' hand chant or a serenade." What peace. When she awoke, she was still humming along not being conscious what she was humming or why. As she recognized the song, and how much she missed her momma's sweet serenade, she tried not to cry. Still, tears welled up in her deep brown southern eyes and one by one, trickled to the apples of her cheeks.

Sissy dressed and wiped the last of the dreams from her face. She headed out of her tent and was greeted by the brisk morning air. She saw Katy at Tom's tent, keeling down getting ready to open it.

She looked over and saw Pati, was frozen as she watched Katy.

"What's Katy doin'?" Sissy asked Pati.

"She's checking up on that weirdo Tom." Pati answered without removing her gaze from Katy.

Sissy turned to watch Katy as she unzipped the lone tent at the far end of camp. Katy leaned over, poked her head inside the tent to find Tom was sound asleep. He was barely breathing.

"Hey Tom, are you alright?" Katy asked. Tom did not stir at all. She watched Tom take shallow breaths. She then reached in to wake Tom with her right hand. She took his foot that was in the sleeping bag and shook it gently and again spoke.

"Hey To.,.." Tom awoke in a rage and from below the sleeping bag lifted the loaded Ruger to Katy's face and screamed.

"You bastard Dog! Die!" Tom's eyes were bloodshot and filled with rage. Katy reached for the Ruger as Tom sent a deafening round out of the pistol. The .22 caliber round grazed the top of Katy's ear as she shoved the smoking Ruger away from her face. The round traveled past Sissy and ricocheted off the hot cast iron frying pan on the camp stove, sending it to the ground in two. Pati screamed. Sissy fell to the ground, but never took her eyes off Katy and Tom. Katy ripped the fired pistol away from

Tom who was now fully awake. His hands trembled. With his eyes wide and unblinking, he stoically looked at Katy.

"What have I done?" He reached out and touched Katy's bleeding ear and watched as blood dripped off of his fingers and onto his sleeping bag. Katy had not realized she was wounded, reached up to feel the warm blood and the sting from the burning flesh of her ear. She glared at Tom.

"What in the hell is wrong with you asshole! You shot me!" With blood on her fingers, she formed a fist. Struck Tom on the cheekbone, sending his head back and down on the padded sleep mat. Katy reeled back and stood outside the tent with the Ruger in one hand the other over her injured ear. Katy began to move towards the camp kitchen. Sissy was still on the ground while Pati peered over the prep table. Both were motionless. Katy saw them both, and called to them.

"Everything is okay, but that son-of-a-bitch shot my ear."
Jackson, Father, Shelby and Curt emerged from their tents.

"What in heaven is going on out here and who the hell is shootin'?" Jackson asked. Seeing blood on Katy's ear, face and hand, Jackson moved quickly towards her.

"Sit down and let me see how bad things are." Katy continued walking towards the camp kitchen.

"That asshole shot my ear. It hurts like the devil, but I hope for his sake it isn't too bad."

"Pati, bring me the horse mending kit and some hot water. Father, Curt, go over and make sure that boy doesn't have any more weapons." Jackson ordered. Father rushed towards Tom's tent. Curt hesitated then looked over at Shelby, unsure if he should follow Father.

"You better go help Father Herrera before that guy hurts any more of us." Shelby yelled out. Curt moved at her order.

"Get out of there right now!" Father demanded. As Tom scrambled to get to his feet, Curt reached in the tent and grabbed Tom by his wrist. He pulled him to his feet, twisting his arm behind him then knocking Tom to his knees as he exited. Immediately, Tom started to plead.

"I didn't know it was her. I thought it was the dogs. They had been chasing me all along the trail and the big gray one was biting me on the leg and that is when I shot at it! I didn't mean to shoot her, but she had no damn business reaching in my tent and pulling my leg."

"What dogs? There haven't been any dogs up here. Certainly not any big gray ones?" Father

Herrera stated. Curt continued to hold Tom as Father questioned him and Jackson attended to Katy's wounded ear. Pati, Shelby and Sissy looked on. Sissy held Katy's hand, winced along with Katy as Jackson cleaned her freshly shot ear.

"That fool could have killed you." Jackson said as he worked on stopping the bleeding. "Take his pistol and lock it up Pati." Tom remained on his knees with his hand twisted and pulled behind him at the hand of Curt's firm grip.

"Honestly, I didn't mean to shoot her. Really, I didn't." Tom stated as he felt everyone's glaring eyes. Katy felt the full effect of the searing pain and yelled out to Tom.

"I was only offering you coffee, making sure you were okay, and shooting me is the thanks I get? Tom, you're an asshole and damn lucky I didn't kill you." Now all eyes were on Katy. They were all surprised by her fortitude and command.

Katy sat on the granite boulder of the fire ring with a cold compress on her bandaged ear. Sissy and Shelby sat next to Katy. Pati was back at the kitchen and listened as Jackson, Father Herrera and Curt had a little 'Come-to-Jesus' meeting with Tom. Their interrogation centered on the supposed dogs, where he was from and trying to figure out what made him such an ass.

"Darlin', you know you're gonna' be fine." Sissy said as she reached out to Katy and held her hand. In an effort to refocus and calm Katy, Sissy continued to hold her hand then asked, "Katy, I'm going to share a very moving and personal dream I had. Would that be okay?"

"Sure Sissy." Katy replied, as she felt the soothing cold compress through her bandage.

"I don't know if it has anything to do with anything, I'm tryin' to make sense of it all. Back when I was just a little girl, my momma had this shiny blue shawl. You know the kind that is all shimmery and soft. Anyhow, she used to hold me in her lap and wrap that shawl around us both and sing her mocking bird song. Before I woke up this mornin' I was dreaming my momma was holding me in her silky shawl. For the first time in so, so many years, I felt like she was right there, holding me. I could smell her soft powder she wore and she had me wrapped on her lap like a butterfly in her cocoon. It was just so real. I looked up to her and as if looking through silken web for the first time I understood that she never left me when she passed on. She's always been there. Peering down on me, her little cocoon, wrapped in her blue silken shawl, all nice and warm and in her arms. When I woke up, I finally realized I wasn't in her arms; there was a moment that was so melancholy. As Grand-Papa used to say, it was bitter as blood." Katy listened intently until Sissy finished her story.

"Tell me Sissy, what was it in your dream that finally helped you understand your momma never left you?" Katy asked.

"It was momma's silver light shinin' down on her silky shawl that was warmly wrapped around me. It was the smell of the powder she wore. But most of all, and this is just a little creepy, but you know that feeling when a spider walks on your skin, it is so light and wispy like light shinin' warmly on you when you're sitting under a big ol' moss covered oak tree? Well, it was in my dream that tingly warm, goose bump feeling her silky shawl made me feel she was right there, holding on to little ol' me." Then softly over Katy's forearm, Sissy mimicked the walk of the spider, light, wispy, while feeling the warmth of her fingers. Right then, Katy understood the meaning of the spiders. They are meant to bring understanding to what she and others feared. All these years, Sissy felt alone after her momma's passing. But the spider in her dream helped her escape the deep fear that she was alone when all along, there she was, living in the spirit of the spider, holding her in the warmth of her silken shawl.

As Sissy told of her dream, the pain in Katy's ear subsided. She now better understood how the spider on the cross represented man's need for balance for his existence. She also wondered what the Washington politicians were hiding and how the spider intended to bring balance to their plans.

24 The People's Congress

Suppose a white man should come to me and say, Joseph, I like your horses. I want to buy them. I say to him, No, my horses suit me; I will not sell them. Then he goes to my neighbor and says, Pay me money, and I will sell you Joseph's horses.
The white man returns to me and says, Joseph, I have bought your horses and you must let me have them. If we sold our lands to the government, this is the way they bought them
Heinmot Tooyalaket, Chief Joseph - Nez Perce

Office of Senator M.C. Phillips. Room 1303, a conference room with massive Brazilian cherry conference table, 13 leather executive chairs, embossed writing pads, silver Waterford pens and crystal water glasses, each filled with ice. Again, the meeting started at 10:01 EST. Senator M.C. Phillips was holding a private meeting; there would be absolutely no record of this meeting. Seated at the table were Congressman George C. Cussler, Senator Claire Holden, the U.S. Secretary of State Margaret A. Vance, and her newly appointed Energy Director, Jack Burton. As usual Senator M.C.

Phillips began her discussion in her expected egocentric and arrogant manner.

"It looks like, *once again*, we have succeeded! We have put ourselves in a very favorable position with the Tribal Councils, our international partners, the NYSERDA and our constituents." Everyone grinned at the Senator, knowing well what lies were beneath the veil of one-sided contracts they designed and carried out. Then Secretary Margaret A. Vance chimed in, in agreement.

"Through the contracts between NYSERDA and the Tribal Councils, we have created opportunities where we get the financial benefit for bringing the Tribe's commodities to our international partners and the Tribes get long term contracts." Again, sly grins are shared at the table. "What makes this so, so sweet, is NYSERDA is responsible for managing the contracts while 19% of the contract funds are distributed among the three off-shore shell partner corporations named in the contract that we control. You all do realize, this will mean over 100 million dollars will accumulate yearly for twenty years. Congress and the Senate establish the rules, and we get the NYSDERA to carry out the directives while we profit and the tribes get nuclear waste securely stored in the salt mines that go in identified as 'Matter of Sensitive National Security' that remains un-scrutinized by the Nuclear Regulatory Commission, the Office of Surface Mining or anyone else, which includes the tribes."

"We are following a long standing precedent as this deal is no different than what congress did with the treaties of 1863 and others. Congressman George Cussler added. "We took land under our divine right of manifest destiny. We did what we needed to insure our interests and for the right people that we wanted settling the West. Again, it was done by the People's congress to secure lands for our enjoyment, our prosperity through eminent domain. Again in the 64' Wilderness Act, we took the very same land and put it to use for a better purpose, our recreation enjoyment. So what, we took it from our fellow settlers. Fuck them, it wasn't theirs to begin with and once again, it isn't theirs. Hell, they got paid for something that was nearly given to them to begin with. Plus we got the Agriculture Department and other land management agencies to carry out the wishes of the people's United States Congress." Then Senator M.C. Phillips continued on the same line of grand-standing.

"Do you recall when our congressional predecessors tied up more land in Utah and Arizona in the 90's where we have vast coal deposits? But remember my fellow leaders; we did it for the

People. So, don't feel too remorseful for all your long hours and hard work, we are only doing what has been and will continue to be our privilege. A privilege and obligation to secure lands, minerals and partnerships for our long-term benefit from lands and resources that we have deemed we are entitled to." Senator M.C. Phillips finalized her oration. Laughter broke out in Room 1303.

"In celebration of this historic and remarkably profitable milestone of our lasting legacy, I am extending a personal invitation to each of you all to my estate on upper east end in Manhattan so we may go yachting on Labor Day to celebrate the labor of others for the benefit of, us!" Senator M.C. Phillips concluded. Again laughter broke out as they dispersed for the day, shaking hands and patting one another on the back for a job well done.

What Senator M.C. Phillips did not know that the Department of Justice had authorized a warrant to allow the CIA to plant microphones and video in her conference room. Each of their Government issued cell phones and office phones of their staff were being monitored to determine how far and who was involved with the Seneca and Oneida Tribes and related dealings. The meeting's recordings were being scoured by CIA Analysts. Intelligence findings were being sent to Officer Nelson for his report to Officer Katy Roberts.

At 05:07 a.m. Katy Robert's watch alarm had gone off for the second time waking her from a deep sleep. This was her alarm to call Officer Nelson.

"Nelson." He answered. Knowing it was Katy. "I have the info you were waiting on and you'll never believe what and who is involved," Nelson reported to Katy as she was waking. "The Senators from New York and Congressman George Cussler, in collusion with the Secretary of State devised a plan to store undocumented nuclear waste in mined out salt deposits on the Seneca and Oneida Tribal lands and they would profit from the contract administered by New York SERDA and…" Katy cut Nelson off.

"But it still doesn't explain the bullets and crosses found at their homes? Aren't there legitimate contracts in place with the Tribes? By the way, it doesn't explain how the bullets and crosses were planted. These were genuine threats made against the most senior government officials and that is why we were called in to investigate."

"True, but there's more. I talked to Ira and the coyote on the cross is a symbol of deception and the bones are of human origin. Ira reasons that the bones are the remains of Native American ancestors used in ceremonies to warn people of wrongdoing and are as sacred as sacred comes. They are meant to bring a certain balance, or as karmic justice to the people they are set upon. In this case, it was our Senators, Congressman and Secretary of State."

"What about the bullets? What is the meaning of the rounds being left?" Katy asked Nelson. "Don't know that one yet, but Ira is working on that as well as forensics, as those rounds are not new and were shot from a weapon with very coarse rifling, the type used in the late 19th century. We're getting deep, real deep." Nelson reported.

25   One Spirit

When we Indians kill meat, we eat it all up. When we dig roots, we make little holes. When we build houses, we make little holes. When we burn grass for grasshoppers, we don't ruin things. We shake down acorns and pine nuts. We don't chop down the trees. We only use dead wood. But the white people plow up the ground, pull down the trees, kill everything. ... The White people pay no attention. ...How can the spirit of the earth like the White man? ... Everywhere the White man has touched it, it is sore.
Winnemen Wintu Woman

"It was real, so real, the dogs had chased me and the big black one had me by the pants and they were getting ready to rip me apart. Every time I shot at the dogs, they would vanish into a gray vapor and reappear somewhere else. They had me and they mauled me. When Katy touched my leg, well I guess I woke up and I was shooting at the dog again and I didn't mean to shoot at her. She shouldn't have reached into my tent. She set me up to shoot her." Tom pleaded his case as any arrogant attorney would. First Tom created a purported reasonable reason to shoot, but accepted no responsibility for his own action. Katy could hear his pleading from afar. She was very angry but also glad the round only grazed her ear.

With Tom's Ruger locked away from his rattled and reckless self, he again pleaded his case to Katy. He offered a back handed apology while not taking responsibility for his own action. Katy was now more interested in his dream than in his half-witted confession.

"So, tell me more about this dog, or is it dogs?" Katy asked Tom.

"Why do you care?" Tom began. Katy glared and tightened her fist in disapproval.

"But if you really wish to know, it started the day I left work. I was riding home on my bike. I was about a block away from my condo and as I rounded a corner, this dark, furry looking dog was right in my way and it nearly caused me to wreck. Then, on my hike just up trail from here," Tom pointed to the trail heading out of camp, "I was nearly to Moccasin Lake when again I was rounding a switchback and there was the dog; the same freakin' dog. Growling, it showed its huge yellow teeth and the hackles were raised. It scared the crap out of me so I backed away from the dog and as I turned to go up trail, there was another one. They had me trapped so I shot at the dog that was up trail from me. When I shot it, it vanished

– Poof!" Tom, now animated, described how the dog disappeared. His hands separated in an outward circular display. "Then I shot at the second dog, and it too, poof, it freakin' disappeared like dark energy." Katy didn't believe Tom.

"Was it a dog or wolf, or was it maybe a coyote?"

"Who gives a rip, wolf, dog, hell, it doesn't matter! Those wild animals were going to maul me!" Tom answered at Katy's questioning.

"Tom, so, what do you do in Portland? And where do you work?" Katy continued her interrogation.

"What does that matter, those animals were going to eat me and it scared me so much, it made me have nightmares and when you grabbed at my ankle, well, I guess that is when I shot at the dog. I mean shot you, accidentally, you know, accidentally." Tom concluded.

"Tom, so what brought you out here? It doesn't seem from your manicured hands and fancy new gear that you actually spend much time out in the wilderness. It seems to me you don't know the difference between say a family dog and a little coyote or a large wolf, do you?" Katy now spoke in a belittling tone, attacking his ego, purposefully getting Tom perturbed. It worked and he fired back.

"Well, I do know it wasn't little fido from across the street. It was big, gray and with a bushy tail." Katy found fault in his story and continued to press him.

"I thought you said he was black?"

"Well, it was black or gray. Hell, what does it matter? Tom retorted.

"It matters." Katy replied. She walked off to talk to Jackson, leaving Tom with a blank stare, wondering why it mattered.

Katy marched across the camp, not saying a word to anyone and approached Jackson who was now with the horses. He was busy brushing out Gray Feather with a stiff bristled brush.

"Tell me Jackson, does Tom's ridiculous story of dogs fly with you?" There is a pause before he answered as he continued to brush Gray Feather, to include lifting his front leg and cleaning out his hoof with his red handled hoof pick. He set Gray Feather's hoof down, stopped brushing, then set the brush and hoof pick down in the olive drab canvas tool bag.

"Katy, where do I begin with you? As I told you before, you need to be careful of what you believe and see out here. Just because Tom saw, in his words, 'a big black dog' it may have not been a dog at all. In truth, maybe he saw something, but he may have seen nothing at all. These mountains are mysterious and filled with the spirits of the ancients and life-forces of the wildlife that inhabit this world."

"But he must have seen or must have been dreaming of something that was attacking him? How else can you explain him shooting me?"

"This place is unlike the city you and Tom are from. In the cities, souls are lost with no connection to Mother Earth. No connection to their ancestors, no relationship with Father Sky. Yes, some say they worship on their Sabbath, but they only perform this ritual for the good impression they leave on their neighbor, not the impression it leaves on their own soul. What Tom saw was 'his truth.' He is afraid of the reflection he sees in his dreams and on his trail. The growling dogs, his tale of being trapped on a trail with two dogs at his heels, the dog biting at his leg. All of that is real. But real only to him as those are the dogs sent by the deceiving Coyote. It is very uncertain that those dogs exist in our sense of our truth. He sees no spider to guide his way out of the shadows and into the spirit light. He only sees his dark shadow dogs tearing at him." Jackson said.

"Jackson, are you actually expecting me to believe that the dogs that Tom has been seeing, in his dream and on the trail are really a reflection, if you want to call it that, of himself? And these, so-called dogs, were sent by a Coyote? Jackson, you are kidding, right? Without pause Jackson continued.

"Every time Tom confronts his dream dogs by shooting at them, they vanish, only to reappear. He has not realized their significance, as you have not realized the implication of the coyote in your dreams."

"What do Tom's dogs have to do with me and my dreams?" Katy was now obviously confused and somewhat angered with Jackson's symbolic references to dogs, spiders and coyotes.

"Cut all the double speak Jackson, I need you to tell me what Tom's dreams have to do with me."

"Your dreams and Tom's dreams have everything to do with one another. We are all connected. We are all one spirit – one interconnected soul you may say. All connected like the flowing ribbons of the river are connected. There are many drops of water, but only one river, one ocean, one Mother Earth. Many people and many dreams make a mighty river of spiritual bonds. Some connect with the people around you. Some may connect with our forefathers and many people looking into our future giving us visions of what is yet to come. Listen and see your dreams. Take heed of Tom's dreams for his are yours as well."

"Jackson, how could they possibly be my own?" Katy asked. Jackson stepped closer to Katy and stared deep into her eyes.

"Do you recall the dream you had night before last. The changing colors of the sky, chanting, spiders, the coyote, warriors, the woman's eyes and the faces of children?" Katy was completely taken aback as he knew exactly of her dream, every detail.

"But how did you..."

"Know of your dream?" Jackson finished her thought. The dream you believed was your dream was my dream, my family, my sky, my Mother Earth, and our children. We have shared a dream. Now, do you see how we are connected?" Katy stood in silence pondering the complexity of the Pandora's Box she had stepped into.

26   Gray Shadowed Thunderbird

The white people who are trying to make us over into their image, they want us to be what they call assimilated, bringing the Indians into the mainstream and destroying our own way of life and our own cultural patterns. They believe we should be contented like those whose concept of happiness is materialistic and greedy, which is very different from our way.

We want freedom from the white man rather than to be integrated. We don't want any part of the establishment, we want to be free to raise our children in our religion, in our ways, to be able to hunt and fish and to live in peace. We don't want power, we don't want to be congressmen, bankers, we want to be ourselves. We want to have our heritage, because we are the owners of this land and because we belong here.

The white man says there is freedom and justice for all. We have had "freedom and justice," and that is why we have been almost exterminated. We shall not forget this.

Grand Council of American Indians, 1927

It was a perfect day for a journey. The plan was to ride out past Alpine Lake, over Glacier Pass and down in to the Frazier Lake area. Have a long and leisurely lunch and ride back in time for a late dinner. Pati had packed everyone's lunch and the riders had filled their water bottles for a long day in the saddle.

As the riders gathered their personal gear for the ride, Tom walked over from his tent to speak with Jackson.

"I want my Ruger back." Tom asked Jackson.

"The day we leave you or the day you leave us. That is when you get it back, not a second sooner." Jackson replied without looking back at Tom.

Uncharacteristically, Tom did not reply. He watched as Jackson mounted Gray Feather and the rest of the riders followed suit. With his double skip whistle, they were on the trail headed east towards the early sun. The morning proceeded uneventfully. They each rode quietly, enjoying the grand vistas, crisp air, and listened to the syncopated clopping of the hoofs against the granite trail.

When they reached Glacier Pass, Gray Feather suddenly stopped cold on the trail. His eyes were wide. Ears perked, he blew hard. He sensed something in the wind the others had not yet perceived. In response to Gray Feather's reluctance to continue on the trail, Jackson quickly lifted his right hand, signaling everyone to stop. He didn't say anything. He stood on his stirrups and scanned the trail and the pass above and saw nothing. He dismounted.

"Gray Feather is sensing the winds and something ahead is warning him not to go on. Wait here." He gestured to Curt to dismount and hold the reins of Gray Feather. Curt dismounted, and held on to the reins of both horses. Jackson proceeded to walk up the trail while they waited anxiously for his return. Ten minutes passed. As the riders talked amongst themselves, Curt kept his eyes forward, looking for Jackson's return. Another ten minutes passed when Jackson came moving down the trail, not quite running, but not walking either. Slightly winded as he approached the waiting horsemen and women.

"The Thunderbird awaits us." Jackson breathlessly reported.

"What do you mean, he awaits us? I'm not going anywhere near that giant bird." Shelby called out. She was still frightened from her previous encounter. Everyone else was waited for Jackson's answer as they felt the reluctance as Shelby.

Jackson understood their apprehension in confronting the Thunderbird again. Jackson then walked over to Katy, took her by the upper arm and started to talk to the nervous riders.

"Katy had a dream two nights before. It was the same as the dream, no nightmare I have every night. We both have seen the crying eyes of Mother Earth and her children. We both have looked at the spirits of the ancient forefathers, praying for the animal spirits to guide us. We have tasted the bitter salt of their tears. The Thunderbird now awaits us to let us see our fears." Shelby, are you willing to let the Thunderbird keep you from facing your fears? Do you wish to be like the masses of lost men and women, willingly ignorant of the truth?

"Jackson, I don't know much about a lot of things in this wilderness. I do know trying to go up against that monster you call a Thunderbird, I simply can't win." Shelby answered.

"How can you win the truth if you don't fight to seek the truth? Listen my friends, I know this is difficult for you to understand, but the mountains and spirits are alive. Face your darkest, most humbling fears and you will find solace because of your willingness to seek your spirit and let it guide you towards your fate. Shelby, be honest with yourself and with the rest of us, what is it that you fear? Instead of Shelby speaking, Sissy explained what she had found in her dreams.

"This morning I told Katy that for many years I'd felt so lonely since my dear momma passed on. It was as if someone came along and took wind from neath' the bird's wing, leaving it to slowly, slowly fall to the rocky ground. But last night as I was dreaming, I realized my momma didn't leave me alone. There she was. The powder and the blue silk shawl she wore were wrapped around me. She was holding on, but I couldn't see her through my own blindness. The spirits of another world, the white silk spider, helped me see my momma again." There was a long pause, and then Sissy continued.

"If the Thunderbird or any monster awaits me, I can face em' because I know my momma is with me. I can be strong to face the darkest shadows that I have." Jackson was impressed by Sissy's willingness to share a very personal and moving experience the mountain spirits had shown her.

"It is not…," Without a sound, the gray shadow of the mighty Thunderbird passed through the group. As if prodded, everyone looked up expecting to see the Thunderbird above them all. Mysteriously, there was no bird. Jackson continued, where he had left off, "whether you find the truth in these mountains. It is not the answers you find that will make you whole. It is your willingness to allow the spirits of Mother Earth and Father Sky into your heart so you can wholly face your fears when they find you. You can rest assured, your fears always know where to find you. Run from the Thunderbird. Hide from Thunderbird, or lie to the Thunderbird that you have no fears. Unless you face the Thunderbird, the Thunderbird will always search for you and ultimately you will need to atone."

Being typically reserved and quiet, Curt spoke.

"All my life, I've always wanted to get away from my oppressive little town. You know, get away from all the things that have let me down including my so-called friends that hang around only to use me. You know, get away from that lousy bar tending job that kept me one step from being completely broke. I've never had a spirit to guide my path, but usually a bunch of no-bodies keeping me down with them. I don't know if I can face the Thunderbird, but if I don't, nothing will ever change. I'll be like Sissy's bird with no wind, always falling, always closer to the rocky bottom. Well, to hell with that, it's now or never for me, Jackson, I'm willing to face the Thunderbird.

Shelby was standing there in disbelief as to what Curt was saying. She was not ready to face this Thunderbird. No way!

"It seems that everyone here except for Katy and me want to go off and face this damn monster bird. But we're not going." There was a short pause then Shelby continued, "I'm not going, no way, no how!"

"Shelby, dear, what are you truly afraid of? Be honest with yourself and with me. Maybe I can help. Maybe between us all, we can help you face what you are truly afraid of." Katy said. Everyone had their eyes on Shelby. She looked around trying to find a compassionate partner to support her unwillingness to face her fears. She found no one. Shelby's eyes began to well up. She tried to form words but couldn't. Curt reached over to her, hiding her weeping eyes from the riders. The gray shadow of the Thunderbird with ominous intensity everyone felt, was nearer than before. Circling slow and methodically hunting its prey. It turned in an ever-tightening circle to identify its approach. From the sky above in the rising thermals, came a heinous, curdling scream from the Thunderbird. It was followed by a loud clap of thunder. The Thunderbird had found its prey.

27   Amelia's Chess Game

Nothing is at last sacred but the integrity of your own mind.
Ralph Waldo Emerson – American transcendentalist

At five minutes before 6 p.m. Gina's phone rang. Gina expected Lisa's phone call. She waited until the fourth ring before she depressed the green flashing icon on her cell phone.

"Hello." Gina answered, knowing well who was calling.

"Hi Gina, Lisa here. I've considered Amelia's offer and I'd like to meet with you to discuss the details. When could we meet?"

"Great. You'll really love working for Amelia. She is very intense and will expect a lot from you but you'll grow to love her. I know I certainly have. She's a real gem. Why don't you come to our office in the morning. You still have my card with my address, don't you?

"Yes, I know your building." Lisa answered. "What time would you like to meet?"

"Be there at 11:00, both Amelia and I had strong feelings you would see things our way."

At 10:49 the following morning Lisa entered the 20-story glass building that housed an array of legal, accounting, and financial services. She took the mirrored elevator to the 17th story, exited to the marbled clad hall that led to large glass door, with the names Newman, Thompson and Wright emblazoned in large gold script lettering. She entered and was immediately greeted by Gerard, a young man in his mid 20's. He was wearing a modern pinstriped suit, vermilion silk tie and the closest shave a man could possibly have. Gerard's demeanor and appearance were reminiscent of a modern eunuch, Lisa thought.

"Lisa. Hi, I'm Gerard." He greeted Lisa as if they were both long lost friends. "Welcome to Newman, Thompson and Wright. Mrs. Newman is expecting you, please come this way." Gerard gestured with his left hand, leading Lisa down a long, brightly lit hall. As they walked, Lisa noticed behind the glass doors the modern and elegant offices with attorneys and legal assistants working in each. They reached the end of the hall, turned left again down another similar, but longer, hallway with more offices. At the end of this second hallway, was a large dark mahogany door with golden raised letters, *Mrs. Amelia Newman, President*. Gerard, knocked twice in rapid succession and opened the door slightly, paused, then walked in.

"Mrs. Newman, Lisa Wyatt, of Cooper & West." He pulled a seat away from the oversized meeting table, directing Lisa to sit, as if rehearsed.

"Will there be anything else, Mrs. Newman?" Gerard asked.

"Please, no interruptions until I'm finished with my meeting. Thank you Gerard." He exited Amelia's office, closing the massive door with a whisper.

"Thank you for accepting my offer, Lisa." Amelia began, as she joined Lisa at the table. She set down a bulky file folder with several bundled documents inside. Amelia opened the folder and the first stack of several was handed to Lisa.

"Here are the terms of our agreement, you can read the details in a second, but in general the contract specifies the terms we discussed at yesterday's lunch. It also specifies what your services will bring to Newman, Thompson and Wright. That being, the information you will secure from Cooper & West. It also specifies your job description, once you arrive at our office and the required attire and code of conduct. I have a call to make while you review the contract. If you find it to your liking, sign the last page and initial the others, where specified. If you have questions, I'll be happy to clarify anything. So take your time, hon."

Amelia handed Lisa a pen, anticipating her acceptance and signature. She left the office to an adjacent library with a smaller yet opulent desk and phone where she placed an outgoing call.

Lisa read the multi-page contract and it did, in impressive detail identify the terms they spoke of at yesterday's meeting. The salary, benefits and a generous clothing allowance she didn't expect. Then came the details she waited to see. The information Amelia sought from Cooper & West were the private corporations they established, including names of corporate principals for the previous six months. It further detailed securing associated contract information connected with each of them. All Amelia wanted were corporations, names and contractors. Simple, Lisa thought. She stopped and pondered the ease of securing this information. Most of the corporate information was accessible through encrypted password by the Cooper & West's management. Where there is a will, there is a way, she thought.

She continued to read the job description. Section 47 specified the assignment to temporary positions to collect and identify data as necessary in association with the organization's mission. The contract ended with the code of conduct, that was impressively detailed, but seemed perfectly manageable. She reached the last two sections where the contract included a confidentiality clause in association with third party contract work Newman, Thompson and Wright performed. It seemed a little odd to Lisa. She figured it was to cover the outside interests not directly associated with the work they did. Lisa signed the last page, and proceeded to the first page to initial when Amelia poked her head out the door.

"Any questions, Lisa?" Amelia asked. Lisa looked up and replied.

"Yes, can you elaborate on Section 47? What do these temporary positions typically consist of? Also, the last couple of pages have a confidentiality clause for third party contractors. Can you clarify the relationship with third parties?"

"I'm glad you asked." She paused, walked across the office and sat across the table from Lisa, she then continued.

"Fact is we contract with the Central Intelligence Agency, the Federal Bureau of Investigation and similar government organizations to secure information when they can't secure it effectively through their operations. Section 47 states that if we need special access to information, you will be used to secure that data. What that confidentially clause specifies is that we cannot release any information under those assignments to other than the CIA, for example.

"What could the CIA possibly want with any information you have?" Lisa asked.

"In your first assignment, it is not what we have it is what you get from Cooper & West. You get the information from Cooper & West and I give it to the CIA. We ask no questions. Is that perfectly clear, Lisa?" Amelia is now staring at Lisa with the intensity of a viper ready to strike at its new found prey.

"Yes. Crystal clear." Lisa replied.

"Welcome to the big league Lisa. I look forward to receiving your information from Cooper & West. After some specialized training, you'll be able to secure information under similar circumstances for our use. Always remember, no phone calls, and data only delivered directly to me. Okay?"

"Yes. Clear." Lisa replied. Finally, Lisa plainly saw her role of playing the pawn in Amelia's chess game.

Lisa slept little that night. She pondered how exactly she would get what she needed from the Cooper & West database. She arrived at work at 6:03 a.m., logged on to her computer terminal and began to search the files for corporations established in the previous six months. The reply she received from her search was, ERROR. Unauthorized access. Password Required. She then searched for principal names, again, Error... She then searched the calendar program that logged all appointments and bingo; the list of corporation meetings began to fill the page. Lisa soon realized the list was really no good. It listed all meetings, not specific corporate filings. She worked on accessing the information she needed until 8:30 a.m. when most of the employees of Cooper & West filed in, including Mr. West.

"Good morning Lisa." Mr. West said as he passed Lisa's desk.

"Good morning Mr. West." Lisa replied, smiling uneasily.

"Lisa, you've impressed me for some time. I've recommended you to Newman, Thompson and Wright, downtown, as they are looking for a new Executive Assistant. I know Tom would hate to lose you, but they need the best and you should look into the opportunity."

"Thank you for the recommendation Mr. West. I'll look into the opening first chance I get." Lisa, still nervous, replied.

"Good luck Lisa. You let me know if I can help you out." Mr. West said as he walked off to his office. "Tom is gonna' miss you!"

Tom! That's it! Tom's original presentation to the president was saved on the corporate server. Lisa forwarded her desk phone to Tom's office. Since Tom would be gone, he had closed the privacy blinds that opened to the hallway, now no one could see her in his office. She entered Tom's office and turned on the monitor, anxiously awaited the access to the corporate drive. As she waited, she rifled though the top, right hand drawer, hoping to find some clue as to his passwords. In this drawer there was tape, staples, a hand mirror, and an unopened fountain pen. It was a cheap China made knock-off, just like the one Tom had given her. That cheap asshole, she thought. Finding none, she started into the second drawer where she found a clean pressed tie, a box of recordable CD's, an unopened box of printer ink and a business card from one of the dancers at The Coco Club, but still nothing. Then Lisa looked in the bottom drawer and again found nothing. The computer was now on with a dialog screen which awaited the username and password.

Lisa switched to the top left hand drawer. Nothing.

"Damn it. What could the username and password be?" She whispered to herself. Well it couldn't be his spouse or kid's name since he hasn't one of either. No dog or cat's name. Lisa paused from her scrambling through the neat drawers.

"Okay, now think like that prick. What is dear to his heart? That is if he had one." Lisa whispered herself. She looked around his office for a clue, anything that may give her a starting point. Then she saw it. Staring over the computer monitor, hanging on the opposite wall is the monochromatic swirling blue self-portrait of Van Gogh. Intense hollow eyes, red orange beard, and if you looked closely, there was a marked resemblance to Tom. She looked the self-portrait and typed into the username on the dialog box, Van_Gogh. Then she went blank. What would the password be for Van_Gogh? She again, looked around for another clue.

"What would that narcissistic ass use for a password?" She again whispered aloud.

As she contemplated the possibilities she noticed Tom's HP financial calculator setting on his desk. It wasn't your typical 1 + 2 = 3 calculators. It was a Polish notation calculator where digits and functions were entered in reverse order. "Reverse order." She spoke audibly. She deleted the user name and re-entered: tombade in the username box and entered Van_Gogh for a password.
ERROR…Invalid username or password was the response on the new dialog box. She re-entered the

password, this changing it to read VANGOGH which appeared as seven asterisks. She was in.

Lisa was a nervous wreck. The ramifications of being caught at Tom's computer securing private client information for her new employer could not be easily explained away. Palms wet with sweat she entered the search criteria for 'New Clients' entered the appropriate date, six months prior and clicked the search function. The server worked. Slow, so, damned, slow. At the end of its search, there, on the monitor were the names of well over 50 new client contracts. She quickly directed the files to be saved to an on-line cloud drive she previously established the night prior. Up popped the dialog box, showing the transfer of copied files was progressing with a display of file folders being twirled and placed into its new found home. RECORDING COMPLETE.

Lisa left Tom's office with both a sense of guilt and success. She resumed work back at her desk for the remainder of the morning. At lunchtime, she verified the saved information was on her cloud drive, made a copy onto a CD. She then stashed it into her purse and took it to her parked car in the employee's parking lot. She placed the CD in the glove box and locked it. She sat and questioned if she had done the right thing. Her hands trembled. The kind words Mr. West said to her this morning. His valued recommendation to Newman, Thompson and Wright, now meant very little.

At 7:53 p.m. Lisa was hard at work on her home computer dissecting the corporate contracts for corporate officer names, and any contractor information. Her phone once, twice and on the third ring she realized it was ringing and answered it.

"Hi Lisa, its Gina." There was a long pause.

"Oh, hi Gina, I, um, didn't expect to hear from you so soon. Um, is there something you need?"

"I simply called to congratulate you on joining our wonderful team. You're definitely a great fit for our company. There was another long pause from Lisa.

"Gina, I'm a…real busy and this isn't a good time. Can we please talk tomorrow?"

"Sure Lisa. Are you okay? You don't sound right. Is…" the phone line went dead. Lisa had closed the line and was back to work. By the end of the evening she had compiled a list of over 375 corporate directors from 57 newly formed corporations.

The following morning Lisa was up early and placed a call to Amelia. The call ended at Gerard's desk, and she left a message on his office voice mail: *Gerard, this message is for Mrs. Newman. Mrs. Newman, this is Lisa Wyatt, I would like to discuss the Executive Assistant position with your firm. Mr. West of Cooper & West referred me to your company. Please call me at your convenience.* She left her cell phone number. Shortly after 10:00 a.m. she received a call from Gerard, at Newman, Thompson and Wright. He said Amelia would be expecting her at her office at 12 noon today.

Lisa arrived a few minutes early to Amelia's plush office. Again, the well-dressed Gerard courteously welcomed Lisa and escorted her back to Amelia's office. As before, there was the double knock on the mahogany door and again he opened the door halfway, paused and then entered the office. Inside awaited Gina, Amelia and a man who wore a dark suit with a blue silk tie, but was obviously not an attorney.

Lisa walked in, and Gina, Amelia and the man in the dark suit noticed her obvious look of distress.

"Lisa, this is Officer Nelson of the CIA. Gina made the introduction. "He has been anxiously awaiting your findings. What do you have for us?" Lisa reached into her oversized purse and took out an envelope, handed it to Amelia.

"This has been one of the most difficult things I've ever had to do in my life Amelia. It felt so wrong." Officer Nelson broke into the conversation.

"Ms. Wyatt, the information you secured for this law firm will help us identify the people that are in violation of multiple Native American treaties. The people who sought to undermine international commerce agreements and are worst of the worst criminals. Without your ability to go beyond the call of duty, we may have not secured the information that identifies the shell corporations and people who directly benefit financially from their crimes.

"Mrs. Newman said we knew we could count on you. Officer Nelson, the CIA, the FBI and the US Department of Commerce have been looking at illegal companies that have been established through false documentation by Cooper & West. They could not secure this information without a warrant, which would have set off a series of cover-ups and people running for legal cover. With this clean data, they can put in motion a plan to snare these offenders at the very game they play." Amelia added to Nelson's kind words.

Lisa sat speechless. She was only starting to realize how much she didn't know about being in the big league of the business world.

28   Deep Investigations

People with courage and character always seem sinister to the rest.
Hermann Hesse – German Swiss poet, novelist and painter

Officer Nelson had immediately sent the list of corporate entities and principals of said corporations and contracting associates that Lisa Wyatt had provided to The Company. Lisa's list of interested parties did not end her involvement with Newman, Thompson and Wright. The CIA needed more. Lisa was politely escorted back to her residence where she promptly turned over the CD that contained the original data of corporate filings. Her personal computer was also taken as evidence to ensure no information went unchecked. Her cloud drive was also deleted and unsubscribed. Again, her involvement did not end there, as she had anticipated. She was taken to the Portland office of the FBI where she was questioned about her knowledge of the contracts, corporate principles and Cooper & West's personnel. There, they quickly identified several names of special interest that needed further investigation.

Included in the list were several defense contractors, lobbyists and members of the U.S. Senate, and U.S. House of Representatives that caught their attention. Again, Lisa was directly questioned as to her knowledge of these companies, lobbyists and representatives by Officer Nelson and an angry looking female FBI officer.

"Ms. Wyatt, tell me about the senators and representatives that met with Cooper & West. When did they first approach Cooper & West to establish the corporations?

"Well, to be quite honest with you, I don't ever recall any senators nor representatives coming to our office. I kept close track of everyone Mr. Bade met with and I don't recall anyone from Washington D.C. meeting with him." Lisa truthfully answered.

"Was there anyone that acted as an envoy to someone for D.C. Ms. Wyatt?" Nelson continued the questioning.

"I really don't recall anyone out of the ordinary, Mr. Nelson, but every once in a while, Mr. Bade would ask not to be bothered. He would be on the phone for over two hours at a stretch. He never said with whom he was talking nor asked for any files to be created before or after his calls. It seemed a little uncommon, but Mr. Bade was so, odd at times, I really thought nothing much of it. I thought it was some long distance relationship, or something personal." Lisa said to Officer Nelson.

"Were these conversations at any particular interval or time of day?" Officer Nelson continued.

"Yes, usually on Thursday afternoon. Right around 1:00 p.m., when I would return from lunch, I would find a post-it note on my phone in Mr. Bade's hand writing and in big bold letters, he always wrote, 'NO CALLS, NO INTERUPTIONS!'" Lisa answered, and then continued. "He would get pretty pissy even if I sent callers to his voice mail, because his phone would make this nearly silent ding sound and he would glare at me through the glass wall. You know Officer Nelson, Mr. Bade is a real prick and I wouldn't doubt for a moment that he would do something underhanded." Lisa concluded.

"Lisa, what else did you notice about Mr. Bade's behavior that you found suspicious or as you stated, underhanded?" Nelson questioned.

"This past spring he went to Europe on what he called his vacation. But I found it very interesting he flew to New Delhi first. He spent only two days there. Then continued on and spent the remainder of his two week vacation in Florence. It seemed odd, but I never questioned him, I merely made the airline and hotel reservations."

"Do you know what he was doing in New Delhi? Nelson asked.

"No. And when he got back, there was about two days in which he was very reserved and spent a lot of time on his laptop computer and on the phone. Again, there were no new clients or files I had to create. It really was kind of odd, thinking back on it. I simply never thought much about what he was doing and I certainly wouldn't question him." Lisa reported to Nelson.

"Do you recall the dates he traveled to Europe and India? Nelson continued.

"It was the first week in April because he was gone during my birthday and all the gals from the office went out that Friday."

"Do you know where Mr. Bade is today? We understand he is unavailable."

"He went to the Eagle Cap Wilderness. He is on some odd solo-backpacking trip hopefully trying to get his head together." Lisa answered.

"Eagle Cap? Hmm." Nelson rhetorically answered. Knowing well that the Eagle Cap Wilderness was also Officer Roberts' current location.

"Lisa, I would like to thank you for your candid answers and I will be in touch with you should I have more questions. I have your cell phone number and I'll be sure you get your computer back as soon as our Analysts are done with it. Do you have any questions of me, Lisa?" Officer Nelson had finished with his questioning and wanted to get this newfound information back to the staff at The Company.

"Officer Nelson, what did Tom do that was wrong?" Lisa asked.

"Well, Lisa, we aren't exactly sure, but it appears Mr. Bade may have been involved in setting up shell corporations. Unfortunately, that is all I can tell you at this point. There is a uniformed officer waiting to give you a ride back to your home. I hope you have a good evening." Officer Nelson stood from the table where they were both sitting, gestured while opening the door for Lisa to exit.

As soon as Lisa arrived home, her phone rang. She was surprised to see the incoming call was from Gina Thompson. She considered letting the call go to her voice mail, instead she answered.

"Hello?"

"Hi Lisa, Gina here. Sorry about the shake down today. It seems that the information you provided really shook some heads. You did a great job, hon!" Gina exclaimed.

"Thanks, I think. Everything happened so fast. It seems like the contracts I retrieved from

Cooper & West really had more than I ever knew or expected to contain. Tell me Gina, what are they really looking for? This investigation is more than shell companies, isn't it?" Lisa asked in utter frustration over the day's events.

"Well hon, I really can't go into the details right now. But we'll be expecting you at our office in two weeks. Amelia has arranged a generous clothing allowance and a spa treatment for you all courtesy of Newman, Thompson and Wright. Both you and I will be meeting with Amelia at 9:00 a.m. on your first day to start you on our orientation program that runs for the first full week then there will be additional training." Gina replied to Lisa, completely dismissing her question. Lisa continued in the same vein of questioning.

"Gina, please. Be honest with me. Is there more going on here with Cooper & West than some shell corporation game? You at least owe me the truth Gina." Lisa asked with intense rancor.

"Yes Lisa, I do owe you the truth. I just can't give you all the details right now. After your orientation, you will further understand what you'll be doing for Amelia and it will also answer many of the questions you have right now. Until then, your questions will have to wait. Lisa, please be patient and trust me, you'll get to know more than you really ever wished for."

"Gina, I do trust you. If anything comes up at Cooper & West, can I call you?" Lisa now feeling unnerved about exiting her position at Cooper & West.

"Of course, hon, you call me anytime. Day or night, buzz me on my cell phone. I'm always here for you." Gina replied to Lisa's request. Lisa hung up the line without even a good bye. She picked up the phone and dialed Cooper & West's business number. There was only a single ring of the phone, and then Lisa spoke into the phone's handset.

"Hi, Lisa Wyatt here. Can you connect me with Mr. West? Thanks." There was a momentary pause as she was connected. Then she continued to speak when Mr. West answered his phone.

"Mr. West, Lisa Wyatt here. I really appreciate the recommendation you gave to Mrs. Newman at Newman, Thompson and Wright. I've accepted their offer and I'll be starting with them in two weeks.

"Well congratulations Lisa. Mrs. Newman called and let me know an offer had been made and you had accepted it. I certainly wish you the best. While Cooper & West will certainly miss you and finding another assistant that is tolerant of Tom's idiosyncrasies will be difficult as well. I'll see you tomorrow Lisa." Mr. West ended the call.

Later in the day, as Mr. West finished a phone conversation, he was interrupted by a knock on his office door.

"Sorry Mr. West, but there is an Officer Nelson from the CIA and he needs to talk to you now." His nervous executive assistant reported. Mr. West's expression was pallid at this startling request.

"But of course, show him in."

"Officer Nelson, CIA." Nelson introduced himself and extended his hand to greet Mr. West.

"Please, have a seat." Mr. West continued. "What seems to be of such urgency that involves my company, Officer Nelson?"

"Mr. West," Nelson getting right to the point of his investigation, "the CIA has found evidence that Cooper & West has been involved in the establishment of certain shell companies for a number of persons of interest and we will require your full cooperation in identifying the persons, corporations and associated involved financiers. The Department of Justice is now getting the necessary documentation for a FBI warrant to secure your company's information associated with those persons of interest.

"Now, wait a damn minute. How is it that you have evidence that Cooper & West has been involved in any unscrupulous undertakings? What evidence do you have to substantiate your accusation, Officer Nelson? Cooper & West prides itself in having a long history of being an upstanding and outstanding firm that would never allow shell companies. Who exactly do you have evidence on that has done such a thing, Officer Nelson? Who?" Mr. West stood with his closed fists square against his rosewood desk.

"Mr. West, it appears at this time that one of your principal partners, a Mr. Tom Bade, has through Cooper & West, set up several companies for agents of foreign nations and representatives of the U.S. Government. Do you have any knowledge of this Mr. West?" Nelson asked.

"Foreign nations? Hell, no. I have no knowledge of this. Mr. Bade's clientele is strictly domestic. He deals with west coast corporations from Oregon, Washington and California. Tom's clients also included a few from other western states, but certainly nothing out east, and undoubtedly, nothing foreign. All of our foreign clients are handled through our subsidiary company out of San Francisco."

Nelson's cell phone rang. It was the call he was expecting.

"Excuse me for a moment, Mr. West. I've been awaiting this call."

"By all means." Mr. West gestured with an open hand to Nelson who promptly answered his urgent call.

"Nelson." There is a minute long pause, as Officer Nelson received the warrant information he had been waiting for. After another strenuously long minute wait for Mr. West, Nelson closed his phone without a word to the caller.

"Mr. West, we've secured and you'll soon be served a warrant for all documents associated with our investigation involving Cooper & West. Can I expect your full cooperation?"

"Officer Nelson," Then there is a long pause before Mr. West continued, "Cooper & West has no intention of hindering the FBI from performing a complete investigation of our firm. We have nothing to hide. If any associate of Cooper & West, including Tom Bade, has any involvement in any fraudulent activity, trust me, we'll ensure the FBI will get what they need." There is another pause from Mr. West. Then he continued. "If Mr. Bade has done anything to tarnish the integrity of this company, I personally, will see to it that he is fully prosecuted Officer Nelson.

"Thank you Mr. West. Your cooperation is truly appreciated. Our special courier should be arriving with the warrant soon. We will need access to your network and some workspace to begin our investigation. The warrant will explain the extent of our interest and I'm sure your governing board will need to see it. One other thing, Mr. West, we need to keep this investigation as quiet as possible as no one will know what or who we are investigating, especially your clients. Understood?"

"Yes. Understood" Mr. West replied. While Mr. West despised the nature of this accusation and investigation, he realized he had little choice if he was to maintain the integrity of his decades of business investment.

29   Spiritual Premonition

What is ominous is the ease with which some people go from saying that they don't like something to saying that the government should forbid it. When you go down that road, don't expect freedom to survive very long.
Thomas Sowell – American economist, social theorist and author

Katy reached out to Shelby and held her hand. "Shelby, we all have our fears. We all have pasts and to free ourselves from what restrains us we need to be willing to accept and face those fears. No one has made it into adulthood without something that scares the hell out of them. No one here is without pain. Fear. Regrets. Even anger. Without those real feelings, we would run headstrong into anything and that wouldn't be too damn smart now would it?"

"Yeah, you're right, Katy. I didn't want to come to this place. I was afraid of being away from the life I like. I am very afraid to take a leap of faith to see the Thunderbird. Maybe it is not my time. I have too much fear to go with you Katy. I knew this trip would be a wild ride, something I've never done before, but really I never expected the supernatural to be so, terrifying and so real."

Curt then reached out to Shelby and touched her shoulder lightly.

"You may not be ready Shelby, but for me it is now, or I'll never have another chance. Katy is right. No one is without regret or anger. I have both and I've got to find out more about the Thunderbird. I want you to come with me so we can find out more about one another. I need you to support me Shelby. Help me Shelby. So we won't have regrets tomorrow."

"How can you be so damn sure we'll even be here tomorrow, Curt? What if that damn monster finishes us off? What if…" Shelby replied but was interrupted by Jackson.

"He will only finish what has already been started. He does not change the outcome of your fears, he simply reveals the your truth to you. Face the Thunderbird, or do not. The truth remains the same. Live with your fears, regrets, anger and your own denial or face them head on and rid the burden you carry. That is your choice Shelby."

"The truth is the burdens I carry are not so heavy. Perhaps I can carry the burdens you cannot Jackson. Perhaps, I don't have anger, regret or sorrow that weighs on the rest of you. Perhaps, I have the strength to endure my load. Maybe someday I will need to look at this oracle of truth, but for me, well, it's not today. Jackson, Curt and Katy, I appreciate what you have tried to do for me. I'm too afraid and just not ready. I don't have the courage and I need to go the other way."

Everyone was silent. Katy realized that Shelby, although naïve had the strength to face her own truth at her own time, it just wasn't going to be now. Shelby walked to her horse, grabbed the reins and walked back down the trail. She was headed to camp where the crazy camper with his evil dog spirits haunted him and where the warmth of Pati's campfire awaited her.

Curt watched in sweet sorrow as Shelby walked, if only figuratively, out of his life. Although she was going down the trail back to camp, she wasn't there to lend support as he thought she would. He felt abandoned. There was a cohesive pause, as they watched Shelby walk down the trail alone. Silently, they noticed as the remainder of the horses knowingly followed Shelby. The remaining riders watched her until she rounded the trail's cutback and the granitic trail dust that lightly billowed from beneath the horses hooves.

"Jackson, do we follow you or we go on our own to the Thunderbird?" Curt asked with reckless abandonment and with the undying sense he had nothing to lose.

"Curt, seeing you have such desire, you lead us up the path to the awaiting Thunderbird. You may be the first to experience his grandeur, or the last or not at all. Only he knows if you are ready to meet your future." With Jackson's blessing, Curt began walking up the trail with Jackson following close behind. Behind Jackson was Katy, Sissy and Father Herrera, bring up the rear, as usual.

They walked for nearly an hour.

"I'd like to take a break for some fresh water at the shady grove up ahead. Is that fine with y'all?" Sissy asked. There was agreement from everyone.

"Why have we not seen the Thunderbird, Jackson? We saw his shadow and heard him back on the last ridge but where is he now?" Katy asked Jackson, as they approached their shaded rest spot.

"Katy, Sissy and Curt, we will see the Thunderbird when he feels you are ready. Katy, do you recall the story that Pati told you about my previous guests, the tribal leaders that prayed with me one night?" Jackson replied as he sat on a large cool boulder in the blue shade of a fir tree. Everyone listened closely.

"Yes, I remember. You were praying and chanting at three in the morning, right?" Katy said.

"Yes, that was the time. The reason they had come was they came to me and told me that the

Thunderbird had been visiting them and they wanted to know why they had been seeing the shadow of the Thunderbird in their dreams. So one night, we had a sweat. We let down our hair to touch the Mother Earth. We prayed and spoke to our Father Sky. We wanted to know what the spirits knew. After many prayers and songs, our ancestors spoke to us. They told of the greed of some people with pale skin and white hair that intended to bring harm to our Mother Earth and Father Sky in the Land of the Seneca and the Land of the Oneida. We asked our ancestors to send a spiritual message to let them be aware of our knowledge of their greed, and their intentions to harm our people and our Mother Earth. They ignored the warnings our ancestors sent." Katy then broke in before Jackson had finished his oration.

"What kind of 'spiritual message' did the ancestors send, Jackson? What does that mean, exactly?" Katy recognized how Jackson's words of explanation had a way of being less than clear.

"Oh, our ancestors work in ways we are always not entirely aware of. What notification they sent is not really of importance. What is of great consequence is that one was sent." Katy immediately countered Jackson.

"What if the people that intended harm received this message you speak of, but did not realize their significance? What if they never realized it was a warning to cease their intended plans?"

"In our world, in the world of our ancestors and in the world of our children, we respect the balance of nature." Jackson answered. He paused as he looked skyward, then continued. "We respect the connection of our spirit with all that is of this earth. In the time of our ancestors, in our time and in the time of our children, the only truth is the integrity of the human spirit. It with the rest of this earth seeks equilibrium. So when an omen of our spirit is sent, it represents the balance of the world and our connection to every part of our world. Do you now see Katy?"

Katy, somewhat clearer, again asked rhetorically. "So if I were to receive an spiritual omen as you called it Jackson, what would it look like? Would it look like a Christian cross made of bone with an etched coyote and a Gila monster? Or like a bone swastika, with a man and a spider carved in it?"

The vivid description Katy offered was more than Jackson could comprehend and he asked. "How would you know of such fetish? Were you the recipient from our ancestors?" Jackson now stood and looked furiously at Katy in a manner uncharacteristic of him.

Everyone else was silent as they listened to the growing tension in the exchange between the two. Katy stood to face Jackson.

"No, I did not receive such a warning, but there were some government officials that did receive such a warning, Jackson. It is my job to figure out why they received this warning and what their warnings meant. It is also my intention to find out why the warnings came with a large bullet? What does that mean Jackson? What does a bullet signify in your world of balance?"

Jackson was now very surprised by the description Katy had offered.

"Unfortunately, Katy, any fetish of any type of iron, such as your bullets, symbolizes the destruction of balance of man and the hope that lies within the human spirit. Where did you find such a fetish? Were they with the other crosses you found?"

Katy calmed, but was cautious in the change in tone of Jackson's questions.

"Yes, they were received together at the homes of two U.S. Senators, a U.S. Congressman and the Secretary of State. This is the reason I am here. To find out what the warnings really mean, who sent them and eliminate the risk they pose to our government officials."

Jackson replied in a calm manner to a clearly distressed Katy.

"Katy, dear, as you proceed in your investigation, please be aware, you are dealing with spirits of immense strength. The warnings do not arrive to these persons without reaching their intended resolution."

"Well what do you mean without reaching their intended resolution?" Katy asked.

The fetish they received was merely the beginning. The spirits have marked your people. They who bring ill to our lands, our people, will ultimately receive judgment for their actions. Sorrow for their families will soon follow. There is nothing that can prevent what has been set forth. No person or spirit can stop what will be. No one." Jackson's face was sadly convinced of this fact and their fate.

The Satellite phone in Katy's backpack buzzed. She removed the phone and walked away from Jackson and the remainder of the group. It was Nelson.

"I finally heard back from Dr. Ku regarding his psychological profile program and the spiritual component is really giving him troubles. Everything he has led him to look at overseas operations in Pakistan and India as the source of the threats. I have a suspicion that this is a red herring which will send our team searching down the wrong trail." Nelson reported.

"Nelson, what I have found out is that the threats to the Senators and others are much more strange and spiritual than we can stop. Dr. Ku's program on psychological profiling is trying to accomplish what the Native American spirits have been doing for centuries. They know who is trying to cause harm to their land and people. The ancient Native American spirits have been able to protect their people and lands by literally cutting off the head of the snake while we chase for its tail."

30   Silky Gray Mist

The discovery of America was the occasion of the greatest outburst of cruelty and reckless greed known in history.
Joseph Conrad – Polish born novelist

Shelby walked down the trail with reins in hand and six horses in her shadow. Slowly they made it back to camp. As she arrived, Pati watched as she meandered alone with the horses following. She rushed up to Shelby and asked in a single breath.

"Where is everyone else? Is everyone okay? Why are you alone?"

"Everyone is alright, really. We got to the top of Glacier Ridge and I realized I was not ready to face whatever they are looking for. The big Thunderbird is out there with them and the horses knew not to go on as well. Honestly, Pati, everyone is going to be okay." Pati was obviously very concerned over Shelby's casual attitude.

"What do you mean, 'going to be'? I'd better go up and see if they need me. Why did you leave them without their horses Shelby? What is really going on out there?"

"Honestly Pati, everyone is alright. We were at the top of the Glacier Ridge and we all saw the shadow of the Thunderbird. I was truly afraid. Jackson explained how the Thunderbird awaits us to let us see our fears, but I was not ready. So I decided I had to come back. The rest stayed and the horses followed me. Jackson let them come. Pati, honestly, they are really fine. If you want to go find them, they are up trail from Glacier Ridge. They are after all with Jackson and Father."

"Shelby, this makes me so nervous. I don't remember a time when something like this has happened. People have dreams. People see things no one can explain, but the Thunderbird is something really new. There must be something bad someone is dealing with. Otherwise, Jackson would never have let the stock come back." Pati said to Shelby.

"By the way, where is that crazy camper, Tom?" Shelby asked after noticing his tent was gone from its morning location. There was no sign of Tom at the camp.

"Funny thing, I told him to come have something to eat. He came over and barely talked. He said he needed to make up for shooting at Katy this morning. He ate a couple of scrambled eggs on a slice of bread then went back to his tent. The next thing I knew, his gear was packed up and he was gone. I thought I would have noticed if he left camp and went down trail. So I figured he left camp in the direction you came. Didn't you see him?"

"Uh, no." I didn't see anyone after leaving the group. Shelby replied.

"What could have happened to him? There really is no other trail except the one you came down on, and I'm sure of that." Pati replied.

"Are you sure, Shelby?" Pati again asked Shelby.

"Yes, I'm sure. That guy gave me the creeps from the first time I saw him. I think I would have been terrified if I would have seen him on the trail, you know, being alone and all." Shelby answered, now feeling as if Pati didn't believe her.

"Something is truly wrong here Shelby. I really don't mean to frighten you, but, something is really wrong. I think I'd better try reaching Jackson on his Sat phone." As she started back to camp, she looked back and realized the Sat phone Jackson typically carried, was stowed away in Gray Feather's saddle bag, which was still on him, here in camp. "Oh, crap Shelby. Jackson's phone is in Gray Feather's saddle bag. I'm going to take Gray Feather and go up trail a bit and see if I find Tom and maybe I'll be able to catch up with Jackson and the group. You stay here Shelby. My Sat phone is just inside my tent in the orange bag. Get it turn it on and I'll call you when I find Tom or Jackson." Pati told Shelby. Pati ran over to Gray Feather, and made a fire-fast mount on to the saddle and was galloping up the trail, not waiting for Shelby's reply.

    Shelby did as she was asked. She found the Sat phone in the orange bag. She turned it on and took a seat on the granite boulder on the fire ring. She sat there in silence, blankly staring at the phone. Hoping it would ring sooner than later. The phone never rang.

    Tom left the camp, intent on catching up with the riders that had left nearly two hours before. Pati had been busy with the morning's dishes and was not paying much attention to Tom after he finished eating and went back to his tent. As she carried on with her camp duties, Tom had packed his gear, and put his backpack behind Sissy's tent, out of Pati's view. He snuck around the back side of the camp and luckily found the unlocked storage box where his Ruger was placed for safekeeping. Tom slid it under his shirt and into the waistband of his pants. He quietly crept back, got his backpack and silent as a worm left camp without Pati's notice.

    He had gone about a mile or so as he followed the horse's trail. Every once in a while, he would have to sidestep the meadow muffins the horses left behind, which once infuriated Tom, now didn't seem to bother him as much. But somehow, deep down, it still did aggravate him. As he reached an opening in the over story of the Fir trees, he noticed the gray dog, or was it really a wolf or coyote, he now gave second thought to, remembering Katy's questioning. Maybe it wasn't a dog, but regardless, he wasn't going to stay on the path and confront this coyote looking animal again.

The coyote looked sharply at Tom as he stood motionless on the trail. The coyote could read his mind. Tom was thinking of which way to proceed to avoid his presence. Tom started moving to the right, staying as far away as the landscape would allow from the staring coyote. The coyote stood still, only moving its head as Tom circled around off trail. Tom could feel the cunning eyes on him and he scurried as he tried to avoid another confrontation. Tom was now looking back over his left shoulder trying to ensure the coyote was far enough away to slow down and again get back on the trail. When he looked back, the coyote was gone. Tom stopped. He looked in every direction and again saw the coyote ahead of him, still far enough to avoid a direct confrontation, but still there. This scared the hell out of Tom as he perspired pure fear. His hands trembled and he understood for the first time the cold vacancy of his character.

He moved up slope cautiously, but quickly. Tom kept a constant vigil on the coyote below. He reached a large grove of trees, and took visual cover behind the first tree he came to. Tom looked back to ensure he was well away from the coyote. But the coyote was not as far away as Tom would have wished. The coyote stood still as he watched Tom. That is when Tom realized he had never seen the coyote move. The coyote was always still. It intensely watched with calculating yellow eyes. Tom ran.

Tom ran and ran until his breath was gone. He stopped to hide behind a massive boulder the size of his office, away from the demonic coyote. He peered around the boulder to see if he had evaded his pursuer, but again the yellow eyes were there. They tormented him. He dropped his backpack, reached down and felt the butt of the Ruger protruding from the waistband of his pants. It gave him a subtle sense of comfort even though he knew it had not been especially effective the times he used it on the 'dog'. Tom stayed behind the boulder until his breath had slowed. He hoped the coyote was far down the slope, he again peered around the boulder to ensure the coyote was still at a safe distance, whatever that really was he did not now know. As he peered out from his cover, a group of five coyotes watched him, crouched, as if ready to pounce. He saw their intense yellow eyes, hooked canine teeth, squat stance, and standing hackles.

"Holy shit!" Tom muttered. He did not wait. He turned to his right and ran as fast as he possibly could. Tom was in a full sprint. He jumped over fallen limbs, jagged rocks as he kept a sharp eye on the advancing coyotes. As he sprinted, moving though the ever-steepening slope, he maneuvered around trees and boulders as he fled. The coyotes seemed to glide as if on ice skates through the forest, coming ever closer to him. They were circling him and he knew he was being hunted. Tom felt as if his heart would burst. Legs burned, he continued to run. He reached for his Ruger and held it firmly with his finger on the trigger. The coyotes closed in as if on cue. He continued his sprint. Running, he looked right then left. He tried to stay, if only a few yards ahead of the yellow canine teeth. As he cleared the latest grove of trees, he looked to his left. He ran at full bore. Then as if in a dream, the coyotes suddenly stopped their pursuit.

31   Religion

Our character...is an omen of our destiny, and the more integrity we have and keep, the simpler and nobler that destiny is likely to be.
George Santayana – Philosopher, essayist and poet

Father Herrera was calm as still water as he watched the shadow of the Thunderbird approach. He knew, as other times in his life, he needed to finally face the truth. After many, many years of waiting, today he knew was his day to emerge out of the shadows of despair and into a new illuminated life. He yearned for the simple years of his childhood. He had been raised in a strong family surrounded by the native culture, the Native American spiritual religion that enveloped every aspect of his being. Then, torn away, to a new way and as he was commanded, to live in the Catholic way. He was now ready to face the Thunderbird after so many years of wretched anguish of living one life, the Catholic way. Which he taught was right and the native life, the way that made him feel at peace, centered and purposeful. He fought with this dilemma for so many years. How could he possibly renounce the great Holy Father, creator of heaven and earth for Mother Earth and Father Sky, the absolute embodiment of everything that is? Father Herrera questioned why was there so much conflict in the two belief systems when at the essence of their teachings shared so much. He sought to answer what it was in the teaching that created so much tension. Was it the paranoia of the Catholic leadership and their insatiable desire for control over money, land and people? Were their holy words of peace hollow when in earnest no greater sin had been committed in the history of mankind than the senseless killing in the name of religion? I am a Christian. This simple utterance has enslaved so many for so long. Why had religion, a simple, yet socially complex mechanism been used to tear brothers and sisters apart? He often questioned the mission of spreading the word of God which had led to the over population of mankind to a point that brought wide spread hunger and undeniable desperate poverty. Why did his Catholic beliefs cross that nebulous line between the teaching of a loving God to thoughts of crimes against humanity? Religion, it is what most people find for themselves in their own time, regardless of its source. People need their own religion, spiritual guidance which leaves them at peace. That much, Father Herrera now understood.

As Father stood there in the glorious shadow of the humbling Thunderbird, he knew it was his time. He looked at Jackson.

"My brother, with your permission I would like to ask my brother Curt and my sisters, Katy and Sissy that stand before me, Mother Earth and Father Sky. And you, my brother of many years, join me in a prayer, so we may have the courage to face ourselves in the presence of the powerful Thunderbird."

Everyone looked at Father Herrera as he was the one ready to lead them in facing the spirit of the Thunderbird. Jackson turned to the group.

"Who will be the first, to join Father Herrera and myself in this prayer?" Without saying a word, Curt raised his hand, followed by an eager Sissy and then an enthusiastic Katy.

"Will you come, stand and face the eastern sky, with the wind to your back and your eyes to your future and pray with me." Father Herrera asked, as he eyed each as they raised their hands in agreement.

"Oh, Great Spirit whose voice I hear in the winds,
And whose breath gives life to all the world, hear me, I am small and weak, I need your strength and wisdom.

Let me walk in beauty and make my eyes ever
behold the red and purple sunset.
Make my hands respect the things you have
made and my ears sharp to hear your voice.
Make me wise so that I may understand the
things you have taught my people.
Let me learn the lessons you have hidden in
every leaf and rock.
I seek strength, not to be greater than my
brother, but to fight my greatest enemy -
myself.
Make me always ready to come to you with
clean hands and straight eyes.
So when life fades, as the fading sunset, my
Spirit may come to you without shame."

Father Herrera finished his prayer and spoke to the entranced group.

"This prayer, my brothers and sisters, I learned from my father, who learned it from his father who heard it spoken by Chief Yellow Lark of the Lakota Sioux. I know in my heart I can face the Thunderbird. I will lead you in our walk through this valley to the blessed waters of Mirror Lake. There we can welcome the spirit of the Thunderbird to free ourselves of the bondage of our past to emerge with a soul of purposeful freedom.

"Father, you have been quite silent though this journey this week. If I may ask, what is it that troubles you?" Katy asked.

"Katy, my sister, what troubles me has burdened me since I was a child. I come from a very different world than yours. My burdens only I can comprehend. As your burdens, only you can understand, for only you have borne their weight. Please, Katy, do not bother yourself with me. Think of what you must face. Many years from now, you will thank me for this. Katy, as expected, wanted to know more.

"Jackson, you said previously that we are all connected. Both you and I shared the same dream. Now Father Herrera believes only he must bear the weight of his own burdens. Father, I know I come from a different world of religious beliefs and a world of hard facts. I realize I don't understand the spiritual world, certainly not in the context of the wilderness and the spirit of the Thunderbird. I, however, do know that if I am going to make it through this experience, I need everyone's help. That includes yours. I also know that you need us in your mission to find the truth you seek. Can I please, with the assistance of everyone here, help you?"

Father Herrera stood in silence as the noblest words came to him from a very unexpected person.

Katy's words touched him deeply and he honestly felt the love and compassion a person could share with another. True, unadulterated words of hope and inspiration he had not experienced since the days of his early childhood. Words he learned from his father when he was taught the power of standing strong against the rain, standing firm against the winds and being proud of the man he was becoming. He had learned the prayer of his Mother Earth and Father Sky and to respect and honor them both.

"Yes, I welcome your open heart to help me and the troubles I bear. Thank you Katy for your words of hope and inspiration as I very much needed them today. You have given me the courage, the hope and the honor to love who I really am. And for that, I will be forever grateful to you all. Jackson watched the people who were once strangers, coming together. Facing their fears and supporting one another, as brother and sister alike.

"Let us head down to Mirror Lake now as we are losing daylight with each passing minute. Father, please, lead us to Thunderbird." Jackson said.

32 Burning Saltbed

Examine each question in terms of what is ethically and aesthetically right, as well as what is economically expedient. A thing is right when it tends to preserve the integrity, stability, and beauty of the biotic community. It is wrong when it tends otherwise.
Aldo Leopold – American author, scientist and ecologist

It was 6:07 a.m. when the gardener at the estate of U.S. Secretary Margaret A. Vance rounded the equipment storage shed. He wore an oversized summer straw hat as he drove the red and black Toro, mowing the expansive lawn overlooking the waters of the Atlantic. He was startled at what he saw. Hung about twenty-five feet above the ground, high in the branches of a giant sycamore tree, was a body. It dripped blood. From his perspective, he was unsure if it was human or animal or why it was hung there. As the gardener drove closer, now with the mowing blades disengaged, he stopped when he recognized it was a human. He rapidly dismounted his mower and ran to the equipment shed where he frantically called the local police.

"Hello, my name is Robert and I'm the gardener at the Vance Estate. Please come quick.

There is a body hanging from the tree on the estate's overlook. Please hurry!"

The Vance estate was obviously well known and within minutes, police squads and an ambulance had arrived. The area was promptly cordoned off with yellow and black plastic crime scene ribbon. Robert was sequestered for questioning. His Toro was riderless, with the engine still idling. Robert was held in the storage shed, questioned and released. The FBI, with the assistance of the local police and coroner's office, were called in. Photos of the skinless body were taken. It was a female, unrecognizable as it hung from the sycamore. The body had been hung not from the neck as in common lynching, but from the hands firmly secured behind the body. More photos were taken of the entire area, including the equipment shed and Robert's truck. Everyone in the household was questioned, except for Secretary Vance, who was reportedly at a hotel in the Washington D.C. area. Every person from the Secretary's staff was called in to be questioned, but Jack Burton was nowhere to be found. He had been last seen at his office the afternoon before and his BMW was still in the employee parking lot.

The assistant to Secretary Vance was contacted in the Monte Carlo room of the Hotel Monaco. When questioned as to the location of

Secretary Vance, she informed the FBI that they had checked in to the Hotel Monaco at approximately 4:00 p.m. the previous afternoon. Secretary Vance was suffering from what she described as a monstrous migraine. The Secretary retired to the Robert Mills Suite at approximately, 4:40 p.m. after an early dinner. At 7:00 a.m. the following morning, after several fruitless efforts, the assistant called the front desk to request entry to the Robert Mills Suite, which she and the Hotel Manager found vacant. The local police were contacted immediately and they called in the FBI who questioned Secretary's assistant. No leads developed.

The body was only identified as a middle-aged female who was removed and transported. But where was the skin and how did the body end up so high on the tree? There were no tracks, foot prints, or broken branches or leaves out of place. The rope was not ordinary hardware store cotton or nylon rope, but rather a thickly woven hemp rope which was gathered as evidence. The skinless bloody body was taken to the coroner's laboratory for further examination.

The FBI confirmed that Secretary Vance was last seen at the Hotel Monaco. They had taken into evidence the hotel's security cameras recording for onsite examination. The Assistant's description was accurate as the video showed she and the Secretary had checked in to the hotel at 3:47 p.m. the previous evening. Video also captured the Secretary entering the elevator at 5:03 p.m. with the elevator stopping on the 7th floor, the location of the Robert Mills Suite. The video clearly showed the Secretary in the elevator. She was grasping her head as if in pain, face lowered. The elevator lights flash to darkness and the remainder of the video showed a vacant elevator. The hallway security cameras and reports from the night security personnel showed little else. Nothing out of the ordinary was seen, heard or recorded, certainly no one exiting the seventh floor at anytime during the night. Secretary Margaret A. Vance had never entered her suite.

It was exactly 3:07 p.m. the same afternoon the body was located when Officer Nelson received a call from the FBI stating that the deceased was positively identified through dental records as U.S. Secretary Vance. She had been mysteriously abducted from her downtown D.C. hotel elevator or hallway at sometime around 5:03 p.m. the previous afternoon and transported to her Manhattan Estate. Once at her estate or at an undisclosed location, her body was removed of its entire outer layers of skin.

The corpse showed signs where a surgically sharp instrument was used from the small of her back and cut the length of her spine to her forehead. From there, it appeared that her skin was violently ripped off as the fascia between the skin and underlying muscle was coarsely torn. It also appeared from underlying muscular tissues of the shoulders and back that she hung in the tree, still alive, for some time before her demise. There were no clues. No evidence and no signs of struggle at the hotel, the estate or anywhere else with the exception of her motionless Swiss wrist watch that was stuffed deep in her trachea, showing the time as 5:03. The remains of her skin were also nowhere to be found. Nor were they ever.

    Nelson didn't waste time after learning of the revolting description of the Secretary's murder. He immediately called Katy, whose Sat phone went unanswered. Maybe the satellites were out of alignment, he thought, tried again with the same result. He then called the Phoenix field Officer, Ben Manuelito. He told Nelson of a seldom spoken of mythical creature, who would take the spirit of the wild animals by taking their skin and mimic them to gain knowledge. Somewhat like a spy that gains knowledge of his enemy by becoming one of them then turning against them with the knowledge he has learned. Nelson thought of what Manuelito told him. He so much wanted to discuss this event with Katy, but to no avail. He waited.

It was near noon. At the moment Nelson attempted to contact Katy, Senator M.C. Phillips had left her D.C. office early, headed for a weekend at the exclusive Viceroy Spa in Palm Springs, California. Shortly after takeoff, the pilot of the executive jet personally welcomed the Senator and her two guests aboard. He informed Senator M.C. Phillips it was only a five hour and 45 minute flight to Palm Springs and a special thank you from Mr. Tom Bade was extended to the Senator and companions as a gift of a most generous supporter, Cooper & West. Before her chartered plane was scheduled to begin its descent, Senator M.C. Phillips excused herself from her companions to the powder room at the back of the jet. After several minutes, her travel companion grew concerned as to her long visit to the lavatory. The plane was to be arriving soon so she went to the back of the plane, knocked on the lavatory door. There was no reply. She knocked again and still, no reply.

"M.C. Dear, are you well?" There is no reply from the Senator. "M.C. are you well?" Still, no reply.

She hurriedly called the steward. A handsome young man onboard that had been waiting on the three ladies and he too, rapped on the door.

"Senator? Please answer me, Senator?" The steward demanded. He received no answer and checked to see if the door was locked. As expected, she entered the lavatory, closed and locked the door behind her. He reached into his pocket and retrieved a slim angular key and unlocked the secured lavatory. He once again knocked as he opened the door.

"Senator?" Expecting to find the Senator unresponsive, he slowly and fully opened the door.

"What the….hell?" He looked over his shoulder to the waiting female companion of the Senator and they both stared blankly at one other. Senator M.C. Phillips was not in the lavatory. She was simply gone. There are two exits from the plane, the main exit near cockpit and one over the right wing. Neither had been opened. The steward ran to the cockpit and advised the senior pilot who then left his seat and went to the rear of the plane to confirm the Senator from New York who had boarded his plane a few hours ago, and whose cackling laughter had grated on him, was not on board.

As they made their approach after their nearly six hour flight to the Palm Springs regional airport, the pilot radioed to the tower of his extraordinary predicament. As procedure required, FBI was called in. Two very unsympathetic agents interrogated the Pilot, Co-pilot, Steward and the senator's flying companions endlessly. How could a U.S. Senator simply go into the lavatory and disappear? They were repeatedly questioned. They took flight data recorders and found nothing to suggest the plane doors opening during flight. The U.S. Secretary of State had bizarrely disappeared.

  As The FBI and CIA searched for the missing U.S. Secretary of State, a call had been received from New York State Police regarding the location of Jack Burton. Two boys playing along the south shore of Oneida Lake, reported finding a burnt body tied to an upright post. They had seen the column of smoke and went to investigate. When the local police were notified and investigated the ghastly murder, Jack's wallet was still in his trouser pocket. The bones of his chard feet lay in the ash of the smoldering fire. There were no foot prints, no signs of struggle, nor any evidence leading to how or why Jack Burton was at this obscure location in New York State. When the CIA found about Jack's demise, his home was searched and they found the same bone cross beneath his alarm clock. It was shaped like a swastika. An antique .50 caliber round was also found in a rarely used watch case which he had inherited from his grandfather. After much research, the Cultural Resource staff person found evidence of similar murders that were recorded by Bartolome de las Casas in 1552. This horrific method of death was used to intimidate Native Americans into divulge the location of hidden gold artifacts. Now it appeared the same method may have been used to extract undeterminable information from Jack Burton, now former Energy Director to the U.S. Secretary of State.

Ten cunning yellow eyes stared down at Tom's mangled body. They had run Tom off a 200-foot cliff and impaled himself on a granitic spire below the fir trees, far below the sudden ledge. The granite spire ripped him starting just above his belt buckle and it finally emerged between his shoulder blades. Bright blood flowed from Tom's mouth and torso, staining the gray granite a glossy crimson. His body hung as if crucified with his spine crooked outward from the gallant stone spire. Tom's Ruger was held tightly in his right hand, but for only a momentary last breath. Only the spirits of ten yellow eyes would ever hear the Ruger tang its way to an obscure crevasse below. At 5:03 p.m. Tom's bloodied Rolex stopped. The spiritual coyote eyes looked down, then all at once vanished in a silky gray mist.

Time would pass and after an extensive search, neither Tom nor his remains would be located. A haphazard wilderness registration was located but offered no clues of his intended destination or expected exit date. His backpack was found by tracking dogs, nearly three miles off course from the nearest existing trail. Strangely, there was no scent beyond the hidden pack. The searchers wondered why anyone would hide their pack if they were lost. Why would anyone be so far off the trail, leading to a remote area of the wilderness, then disappear as if he had stepped off the edge of the world into oblivion.

Months later, when Tom's brother from Seattle and his sister from Santa Fe were trying to come to terms with his disappearance, would they find a little white cross among his Rolex watches, platinum tie pins and diamond and gold dinner ring. They found the cross interesting, but it seemed somehow insignificant. All of Tom's possessions were placed in labeled boxes by a moving company and transported to a storage facility where it lay in wait in their hope of Tom's eventual return.

Three hundred and sixteen miles East of Palm Springs, in the Wingate wash salt flat in the hell-hot misery of Death Valley was Senator M.C. Phillips.

BLANKET OF DECEPTION

She awoke from what she thought was a dream. In reality, she awoke into her ultimate nightmare. She had been stripped nude and she was laid spread eagle, with her face towards the burning sun. The dry 125 degree air she breathed was suffocating. She tried to move but was unable to break free of her shackled position. She had been tied with wetted rawhides which were left to dry and constrict at the wrists, elbows, neck, knees and ankles. The once honorable Senator M.C. Phillips was immovably staked to the burning saltbed. She screamed as the platinum and diamond wristwatch burned her strangulated wrist. The watch read 5:03 p.m. The echoes of death called back. She had absolutely no idea where she was or how she had come to be there. The last thing she recalled was having a bit of a headache developing and had excused herself to the airplane's lavatory to take a dose of aspirin, and then her world went black. She lay in the consuming sun, blistering, burning for what seemed like an eternity. Within three hours, the shadow of the arroyo wall shaded her blistered face and body. Slowly, the evening shadows covered her, but she was still shackled to salt's deathbed. As evening wore on, she felt as if she could regain her strength from the day's heat and free herself. As twilight started and the stars began to appear in the clear aquamarine sky, out came the desert ants. Not tens, not hundreds, but tens of thousands of desert ants, climbing her naked, blistered and oozing body. She screamed with a fear that lies in the deepest crevice of human thought. This time, there was no echo of death, only the dark, vacant silence of her departed soul.

By dawn, there were only a few straggling ants, a few iridescent colored flies, the remains of a full skeleton wearing a shining platinum and diamond wristwatch. Missing was the right leg below the knee and above the ankle as an unknown carnivore tore away with it. The rawhide and wooden stakes buried deep in the salted ground remained as well. The next morning, from sea to shining sea, every news channel and paper reported the story of the missing Senator M.C. Phillips, of New York who stepped into a privately chartered plane from D.C. to the resort in the sun. Time and creatures of night took M.C. Phillips bit by bit into the underworld of the one of the most hellish place on earth, a suitable location, chosen by the demonic nature of her soul.

As expected, chaos ensued at the CIA and FBI and was the talk of Washington as they became aware of Secretary Vance's grisly murder that had happened hours before the disappearance of the Senator M.C. Phillips. The CIA brought in for safe holding Congressman George Cussler and Senator

Claire Holden whom had previously received the unusual rifled bullets. The CIA and FBI struggled to determine how these women who they thought were safe could meet horrific and mysterious circumstances. There were no answers and no organizations claimed responsibility for their demise. The only clues were the strange crosses, antique rounds that created more obscurity, and raised more questions than answers. The report from Officer Katherine Roberts that was in the Eagle Cap wilderness only added more questions to the peculiar circumstances.

Senator Cussler was sequestered to an undisclosed location in a secure underground facility associated with the Pentagon. The location he was being held for his security and safety was five levels below ground in a structure designed to withstand the most audacious nuclear bombings. His living situation was far from the dreary 60's pulp fiction films of steel bed frames in dormitory style living. The senator was housed in a spacious suite-like room with natural light fixtures, and video conferencing, so he could remain engaged with his office staff. Multiple levels of security were utilized to ensure his complete safety. There were four-assigned security personnel to provide comfort and continued communication with his constituency. Still, he wasn't content.

Senator Claire Holden, a recipient of death's calling card, was also sequestered. Her location of choice was removed from the obvious Washington fallouts. She was flown to The North American Aerospace Defense Command (*NORAD*) facility in Colorado. There she was shuttled with her family to an underground location where she would wait out this unusual and horrific crisis. No leads, no answers, no news came to the restless Senator. The wait continued.

Still 48 hours after the corpse of Secretary Vance was found there were no clues, except for the newly discovered body of Jack Barton. Senator Claire Holden, in a one sided conversation with the CIA's Director of Terrorism Analysis, Mark Kelley, tore at his inability to provide her the answers she sought. Eventually, after fifteen minutes of berated remarks, the Senator hung up in frustration and true fear as she had never felt. This all started with strange iconic figures appearing then suddenly, manifesting in grotesque torture and a strange circumstance of disappearance from an airplane. Still angry, she sat at the foot of her bed, trembling and sweating in unrestrained fear. She called for her assistant that was in the adjoining room who suggested a visit by the staff physician. The doctor prescribed a mild sedative to help her growing sense of dread. The rest of the evening, Senator Claire Holden remained in her secure bedroom, reading and occasionally talking via videoconference with her Chief of Staff at her New York office.

It was 4:30 a.m. the following day when the side table alarm sounded, which awakened Senator Holden's assistant. She got out of bed to ready herself for the day's work. At 5:00 a.m. she heard the alarm in the Senator's bedroom sound. The Senator did not mute the alarm as it buzzed. Senator Holden's assistant went to her door and knocked. She could hear the Senator talking in the adjoining room in a muffled tone. Not unusual for this early hour she thought. This time she listened with greater attention as to the context of the ongoing conversation. She could clearly hear the rambling words of Senator Holden.

"yew – two – sky – must – speaker – over – treat – line – policy – the – enter – ocean – earth – repeat - code – well – up – fire – it – option – Wednesday – is – federal – guide – borrowed – sorrow – animal – from – spider – where – our – air – plate – children – did – void – yew – two – earth – must..."

The assistant, listened for a minute as the Senator, carried on repeating words that made no sense what so ever. At 5:04 a.m. she called security without disturbing the Senator and requested they call in the physician as well, as something was very, very wrong with the articulate Senator Holden. The doctor was first to enter her bedroom where he found the Senator, sitting on the foot of her bed. She wore her pajama pants, one of her best dress shoes, an inside-out jacket put on backwards, as she looked mindless into the dresser mirror opposite of the bed. With the alarm clock abuzz, the Senator repeated, without end, without response to the doctor as he asked questions of her.

"yew – two – sky – must – speaker – over – treat– line – policy – the – enter – ocean – earth – repeat - code – well – up – fire – it – option – Wednesday – is – federal – guide –borrowed – sorrow – animal – from – spider – where – our – air – plate – children – did – void – yew– two – earth – must…."

She repeated the words endlessly. She was again administered a sedative and dozed off for two hours and when she awoke, she continued with the same deranged ramblings.

Back at The Company, Director Mark Kelley called Officer Katy Roberts to inform her of the latest with the Secretary and Senators. She answered her phone, only to reveal to Chief Kelley news that sent Washington into a wild spin.

Congressman George Cussler was scared as hell when he heard the news of Senator Claire Holden. Even in one of the most secure places on earth, there was no stopping the wrath that awaited Senator Holden. As Congressman Cussler was briefed on the events, there was a call to his secure location. Chief Mark Kelley needed to speak to him urgently. With the assistance of his aide, he was connected in the video conference room. He looked tattered and distraught at the news of his peers. Director Kelley noticed the Congressman appeared to have aged nearly a decade overnight. Mark Kelley opened the conversation with Congressman Cussler.

"Congressman Cussler, thank you for your time. We are in need of some urgent information from you and we also have some important news you need to be aware of."

"Yes, first of all, what important news do you have? Do you know who is committing these murders and poisonings?" Congressman Cussler asked.

"Actually, yes." Director Kelly promptly answered.

"Well, who damn it, who? Have you caught them?" Congressman Cussler demanded.

"According to our Officers, it appears that Secretary Margaret A. Vance in association with Senator M.C. Phillips and Senator Claire Holden and most likely members of their staffs have been involved in a conspiracy against the Seneca and Oneida tribes in your home state. Were you aware of this Congressman Cussler?" The red angry color from the Congressman's face faded. He became ashen, his blue eyes vacant. Chief Kelley continued.

"There are countless contracts and business filings emerging which implicate you in this conspiracy and this is where we believe you can bring some clarity to deaths and the unresolved state of Senator Holden. I do want to be clear with you Congressman. Time is of the essence and what information you share with me will be recorded as part of our investigation, but it may also save your life. Is this clear, Congressman Cussler?" Director Kelley concluded. There was a long and desperate pause. Congressman Cussler thought of all the implications of the words he would utter. His empty eyes and ashen face on the video monitor captured his condition. His hands trembled and voice cracked as he attempted to misinform Director Kelly of their magnanimous deception.

"Director Kelley, the contracts we entered into with the Oneida and Seneca were never intended to bring harm to anyone. It was Senator Phillips and Secretary Vance who brought us this opportunity for the tribe's economic future. It was that simple, Director Kelley. It was good for their economy. There was nothing more to it than that. We did nothing out of the bounds of our authority. Nothing." The Congressman concluded.

"Sure, Congressman Cussler, sure." Director Kelly replied.

"Director Kelley, you have no right to speak to me in that belittling tone. Listen, we did nothing wrong, Damn it!"

"Congressman Cussler, maybe you can enlighten me on how your agreements included the use of underground mined areas as storage facilities for nuclear materials from countries abroad without the expressed knowledge of neither Congress, our oversight departments nor the Tribal Nations of the Oneida and Seneca?"

"Nuclear storage? Whatever do you mean Director? I have no knowledge of nuclear storage from Pakistan." Congressman Cussler proclaimed.

"Congressman Cussler, I never mentioned Pakistan. How did you know the nuclear materials were from Pakistan?" Director Kelly asked.

"But,..." Congressman George Cussler began to say when he was interrupted.

"But you have not been entirely honest here, Congressman. I know about your plans with China, India and Pakistan. I also know of the shell corporations that were established to funnel nineteen percent of the profits to you, the Senators and Secretary Vance. I also know what caused the demise of your respected peers and..." Director Kelley was now the one being cut off, at mid sentence.

"What do you mean by 'what' caused their deaths? You mean who, don't you?" Congressman Cussler asked.

"Congressman Cussler, it was not a *who* but it was a *what*. And what have reportedly killed them were their own actions brought upon the lands and spirits of which you were planning on inflicting through your deceptive contracts. Truth is, Congressman, no one was able to save any of them, and we are unable to guarantee your safety. At 14:00 hours a security detachment with the FBI, Officer Nelson of the CIA, an attorney from the Department of Justice and your attorney will arrive at your location. At that time, to begin with, you will be charged with two counts of conspiracy against foreign nations. Other charges will be pending as more evidence is gathered. Until that time, you will remain under arrest at the location you are currently housed. Security has been informed. The only contact you will have out of the Pentagon's secure facility is on a secure phone line to your attorney. Have a good day, Congressman Cussler." Director Kelley ended his conversation with the Congressman and closed the video feed leaving the now former Congressman George Cussler expressionless. His world of power, prestige, and entitlement had instantly vanished.

At 9:00 a.m. the pressroom at the Department of Justice opened. The Attorney General stood at the podium and Director Kelley stood behind him and to his left. The Attorney General read from his carefully prepared and rehearsed notes:

```
"Ladies and gentlemen of the
press, thank you for being here
today. The Department of Justice in
cooperation with a special
investigative unit of the CIA and
the FBI have been investigating the
recent death of U.S. Secretary
Margaret A. Vance at her estate in
Manhattan; the unresolved and
mysterious disappearance of Senator
```

M.C. Phillips of New York; and the possible poisoning of Senator Claire Holden, also of New York. Also investigation is underway in the death of Jack Burton, Energy Director, with the U.S. Secretary of State's office. These investigations are ongoing and further information will be forthcoming as events unfold.

As part of this investigation, with the assistance of our Field Officers in Oregon, Arizona and in Virginia, we have discovered a conspiracy involving the four persons previously mentioned plus Congressman George C. Cussler of New York, 47th District. Emerging evidence points to the Secretary, the two Senators and the Congressman and specific members of their staffs had conspired with official representatives of China, India and Pakistan in an effort to contract the illegal disposal of nuclear waste at two subsurface mining facilities on treaty lands of the Oneida and Seneca tribes of

New York. This conspiracy to illegally use foreign lands for their personal financial gain also remains under investigation and again more information will be forthcoming as the investigation proceeds.

    Being that four of the main conspirators have met their demise, missing or mentally incapable to understand these charges, the DOJ is proceeding to charge Congressman George C. Cussler of New York with conspiracy to commit crimes against foreign nations, that being the tribal lands of the Oneida and Seneca. Persons of interest remain under investigation and further charges are pending awaiting results from this investigation. Congressman George C. Cussler is being held at an undisclosed location for his safety and will be charged with previously mentioned crimes at 14:00 hours Eastern Standard Time. Thank you."

Every hand of the press corps was raised when the Attorney General finished. Director Kelley then stepped to the microphone.

"We will not be taking questions at this time until further information develops from the investigation. Thank you for your patience." He left the podium, again, with all hands of the press corps raised and questions being barked out.

As promised, at 14:00 hours, Officer Nelson, the prosecuting attorney from the Department of Justice and Congressman George Cussler's attorney met and the Congressman was charged. They brought him into a near vacant office with a large stainless steel conference table where he heard the charges he now faced. He sat stone faced, facing the charges alone. Only Congressman George Cussler would face criminal prosecution. The other four had already faced a greater penalty. They were served a just sentence the spirits brought upon their deceitful souls.

After being charged the Congressman was eventually prosecuted for many crimes, along with eleven congressional staff. His title of Congressman was stripped along with privilege and benefits. He was incarcerated, humiliated and eventually brutally assaulted by other prisoners. Convict #61709 of the Ray Brook Federal Correctional Institution endured for twenty seven agonizing months. On a cold January morning he was found in his cell, hanged. Not from his neck as one would surmise, but was hung from bound wrists tied at the back as Secretary Vance was found. His mouth stuffed with owl feathers, which had muffled his screams. Found in his back were 503 spines from the desert cholla cactus deeply imbedded into his spinal cord. At the base of his neck was an imbedded swastika fetish made of bone, symbolizing the balance and order from the spirit world had returned.

Senator Claire Holden, of New York, was deemed mentally unfit to stand trial unlike the Former Congressman George Cussler. She was eventually committed to the State of New York hospital for patients with severe mental illness. It was at this facility where another patient who spent time in the same ward with the former Senator finally understood what she was saying. Former Senator Holden was repeating a lesson she was never to forget. The mental patient informed the attending nurse.

"If you listen to every third word, and ignore the others and it makes sense:

"<u>you</u> – two – sky – <u>must</u> – speaker – over – <u>treat</u>– line – policy – <u>the</u> – enter – ocean – <u>earth</u> –

repeat – code – <u>well</u> – up – fire – <u>it</u> – option – Wednesday – <u>is</u> – federal – guide –<u>borrowed</u> – sorrow – animal – <u>from</u> – spider – where – <u>our</u> – air – plate – <u>children</u> – did – void – <u>you</u>– two – earth – <u>must</u>..."

    This information never did go beyond the walls of the mental hospital.

33   Blessed Waters

Nothing in life is to be feared, it is only to be understood. Now is the time to understand more, so that we may fear less.
Marie Curie – Polish chemist and physicist

Father Herrera had led the group of five to the placid mountain waters of Mirror Lake. On the far shore of the lake was a large stand of fir trees and large glacier carved granite monoliths the size of a two-car garage. The incoming water to the lake flowed down a stream of boulders that created a soothing, bubbly white noise. On one of the massive rounded monoliths, perched the Thunderbird. He waited and watched with blood red eyes and giant talons of carbon black steel. The Thunderbird appeared to await Father Herrera's lead.

"Stand with me, with your feet in the waters of your fear." Father Herrera spoke as he walked towards the Thunderbird. They all joined hands, and walked in joined steps into the cold waters of Mirror Lake. Sissy was trembling. Katy had never felt such power; such an aura of spiritual intensity. Tears flowed as she faced Him. Curt entered the frigid mountain lake, but as he watched the Thunderbird, a sense of peace and strength overcame him. As for

Jackson, the magnificent bird once again, as in his childhood, gave him an intense feeling of both fear and strength, perhaps the balance of his life force. They stood and watched the Thunderbird above his rock perch. He stared down through them. He examined their awaiting souls. Then the Thunderbird with intense vigor and power spread his massive black wings and shrieked so loudly causing the water of the lake to create a wave which splashed on the waiting souls. The burning red eyes never turned away. Everything went pitch black and a hypnotic sense of vertigo overcame them all. They felt as if they were being spun through the air. They were tumbling, turning, spinning uncontrollably, and violently shaking as if experiencing a horrific plane crash. The odors of whiskey, vomit, and urine filled their noses. Nauseated and unbalanced, the group remained, holding hands. Unexpectedly, everything in landscape turned an electric shade of indigo. The truest blue of heaven anyone could ever imagine. The lake's waters, the trees, the Thunderbird and their auras were aglow. In that flash of brilliance which seemed to last half a minute, everyone of the group saw within themselves the hope, courage, freedom, honor, duty, mercy, which was contained in their souls. Their fears and burdens had been lifted and a true sense of self emerged. The light faded from indigo to a soft pale blue and gradually faded away. They all instinctively turned and emerged from the lake water. There was calm in the air they all felt as they stood in silence. The Thunderbird was only to be seen flying away, high in the drifting winds. Father Herrera was the first to speak.

"My friends, you have stood with me in the presence of a great power. For I have seen my new path in life. I no longer have the burdens of my past. I can now face my ancestors with a clear and open heart." Father Herrera paused, and then continued. "Curt, please share what you have experienced in the presence of the great Thunderbird." For the only time in his life he felt an odd weightlessness about himself.

"Father, I have seen the courage, the potential and I too, have seen my calling. It was as if I could see into the future. It was so incredibly...vivid and real."

"You know," Katy jumped into the conversation, "you're right Curt. It was as if I could see into the future, but strangely enough, I could also see to the past. Not only my past, but the past of others. How could that possibly be Jackson?" Katy asked.

"It is as I previously said. We are all one. Like flowing ribbons of water of the river are connected. There are many drops of water, but only one river, one ocean, one earth. There are many dimensions to this world and the Thunderbird helped you see what is in your soul. Tell me Katy, what visions did you have? Jackson asked.

"I was standing in a clearing of a wide meadow. But I was not looking through my eyes. I was looking through the soul of the woman that was in my dream. It was a Native American woman, whose children were being slaughtered by men on horseback. I could see the spirits of Mother Earth. I could see the Senator M.C. Phillips meeting with all the Washington people, scheming to rape the lands of the Oneida and Seneca. I could see the ancient spirits, entering their homes and leaving the carved bones of their ancestors. Leaving the very bullets that killed their children in the homes of those manipulative men and women. But I could also see myself, my future. I was, or should I say will be in a prayer circle with many women and men. The cottonwood and rawhide drums making the earth tremble. I saw myself very much at peace with the world and people that I am with. Interesting thing Jackson, you were sitting opposite of me in the prayer circle, and you were beating a drum with a small boy at your side. Who could that child be, Jackson?" Katy asked.

"Katy, that child is yours, of course." Sissy said.

"Mine?" Katy questioned.

"But of course, Katy, every child needs a good mother and a good teacher. I still have my mother, just not in this world, but she is here." Sissy touched her chest above her heart. "I know I'm going back home to Savannah and be the best soul singer, the best teacher and the best momma my town has ever known. I've seen it now I can go do it."

Katy stood there with her mouth agape. She too had seen Sissy, on a stage lit with sunset orange lighting and in the front row a handsome man with a little girl on his lap, swaying to Sissy's soft sweet song. But Sissy already knew that.

"Jackson, what vision did you have? Where did the Thunderbird lead you?" Katy asked.

"The wise Thunderbird led me here many years ago. I feared him as I was beginning to think there was to be a new calling. The Thunderbird has once again confirmed these mountains will always be my home. At my end, my spirit will remain here with all the spirits of my ancestors. Today he has confirmed that my true calling is to help those find their genuine heart. I saw myself standing in the open meadow in the presence of Mother Earth while I prayed to Father Sky. I prayed for our connection to one another as a people of this beautiful earth.

As they turned to head back on the trail, Katy glanced down at her watch. They had been at Mirror Lake for not just a few minutes, but several hours. As they crested the trail they met up with Pati. They walked back to camp where Pati and Shelby prepared and served a Dutch oven dinner. They all sat and recounted their experience and how they each had similar, but different experiences in the presence of the Thunderbird.

After returning home, Father Herrera decided to leave the teachings and doctrine of the Catholic Church which angered his Archbishop. After a time of reflection, he returned to his native home and became an active leader in his Jicarilla community. In time Father Herrera became a respected elder. Every so often, he would find himself back in the Eagle Cap Wilderness with Jackson, the spirits of the mountains, Mother Earth and Father Sky, delving ever deeper into his soul and seeking continued understanding.

Following her wilderness trip, Shelby did not find her calling but respected and valued what the mountain brought. She willingly returned the following summer to continue her growth. Little by little, she began to see herself in an entirely new light. She saw herself as selflessness and a part of the vital human potential. She grew to be purposeful, proud and honorable as the mountain had taught her.

Curt, after returning to his home town for a short time, made good on his word to his coworkers at the bar. By October he had packed his belongings into his old truck and left to live on the edge of the Eagle Cap Wilderness to keep connected to his new found spirit. Today he resides in Joseph, Oregon.

Sissy and Katy traveled east together and went their separate ways at Atlanta's Hartsfield-Jackson International Airport. Sissy flew back to Savannah to the roots of her music and revived the old southern soul music. Three years after her wilderness trip she was married to the bass player of her band and they had a little girl, Katy Bird Samuels. Sissy and Katy remained lifelong friends.

Katy, after finding out how the spirit world and the western world were at polar ends of understanding one another, left the CIA to learn of the spirit world. She eventually settled, living near Father Herrera in Dulce, New Mexico and the ancient spirit world. She used this newfound knowledge to help the leaders of western world respect all cultures, their values and diverse knowledge.

Two years passed when the CIA was once again brought into the fray when they are consulted about the Chinese, Indian and Pakistan government leaders who are found with strange bone crosses imbedded below their skin. – no scars, merely the obvious swastika outline as a reminder of where not to tread.

*Humankind has not woven the web of life.
We are but one thread within it.
Whatever we do to the web,
we do to ourselves.
All things are bound together.
All things connect.*

Chief Seattle, Dwamish - Sugampsh

-END-

Made in the USA
Charleston, SC
12 January 2013